# Ninefox Gambit RPG

## Yoon Ha Lee

Android Press

Copyright © 2023 by Yoon Ha Lee
Cover Art by Stephanie Folse
Scenarios written by Marie Brennan

Published by Android Press
Eugene, Oregon
www.android-press.com

ISBN: 978-1958121443

All rights reserved. No part of this book may be reproduced in any manner whatsoever without written permission of Android Press, except in the case of brief quotations embodied in critical articles and reviews. Please respect the rights of the author and the hard work they've put into writing and editing the materials in this book. Do not copy or distribute, and do not post or share online. If you like the book and want to share it with friends, please consider buying additional copies.

*For Chris Chinn. This game is for you—without your help, encouragement, and mentorship, I would never have gotten this far. May the dice gods smile upon you!*

# contents

| | |
|---|---|
| NINEFOX GAMBIT RPG | 1 |
| INTRODUCTION | 2 |
| WHAT THIS GAME IS ABOUT | 3 |
| SETTING NOTE | 5 |
| SAFETY AND RELATED CONSIDERATIONS | 6 |
| SPECIAL CONTENT NOTE | 8 |
| HOW TO PLAY | 9 |
|   GROUP GOAL | |
| SUMMARY OF CHARACTER CREATION | 11 |
| FACTIONS | 14 |
|   ANDAN | |
|   KEL | |
|   NIRAI | |
|   RAHAL | |
|   SHUOS | |

VIDONA

PERSONAL TRAITS ............................................. 27
   PERSONAL TRAITS: EDGES
   PERSONAL TRAITS: HERESY
   PERSONAL TRAITS: COMPLICATIONS
   SIGNIFIERS
   ON DISABILITY AND PERSONAL TRAITS

LOCATION TRAITS ............................................. 30

CLOCKS ............................................. 31
   PERSONAL CLOCK
   PARTY CLOCK
   HEXARCHATE CLOCK

CHECKS AND TAGGING ............................................. 34
   INDIVIDUAL CHECKS
   ROLLING 6's
   GROUP CHECK
   OPPOSED CHECK

COMBAT ............................................. 39
   PHYSICAL COMBAT
   EDGE COMBAT

HEALING AND RECOVERY ............................................. 43

MONEY AND RESOURCES ............................................. 44

ADVANCEMENT ............................................. 46

GUIDE TO GAMING ............................................. 48
  Safety.
  Setting the party up for success.
  Setting individual characters up for success.
  Character Death.

Assimilation vs. Rebellion.
NPCs.
Setting.
Items.
Mass combat and space battles.

## SAMPLE CHARACTER SHEET — 53
### EXAMPLE CHARACTER

## ONE-SHOT ADVENTURES — 56
By Marie Brennan
### INTRODUCTION

## 1. A HERETICAL SACRIFICE — 59
Overview
Setup
Development
Crisis
Variations
NPCS
PRE-GEN PCS

## 2. POISON FROM WITHIN — 68
Overview
Setup
Development
Crisis
Variations
NPCS
PRE-GEN PCS

## 3. THE FIELD OF DIPLOMACY — 77
Overview
Setup

    Development
    Crisis
    Variations
    NPCS
    PRE-GEN PCS

**APPENDIX A: CALENDRICAL TRAITS (OPTIONAL RULE)** — 88

**APPENDIX B: AN OVERVIEW OF THE HEXARCHATE** — 91
    HIGH CALENDAR
    REMEMBRANCES
    FACTIONS
    ANDAN
    KEL
    LIOZH
    NIRAI
    RAHAL
    SHUOS
    VIDONA
    CULTURE
    LANGUAGES
    TECHNOLOGY

**APPENDIX C: THE HEPTARCHATE** — 103
    LIOZH

**APPENDIX D: FIGURES FROM THE HEXARCHATE** — 107

**ACKNOWLEDGMENTS** — 130

About the Author — 131

# NINEFOX GAMBIT RPG

By Yoon Ha Lee
with Scenarios by Marie Brennan

# INTRODUCTION

You are a citizen of the Hexarchate, a tyrannical empire that spans countless systems and star fortresses. The vast majority of the population labors under the rule of six Hexarchs and the factions they control. In exchange for power or prestige, you've joined a faction yourself.

These truths you know:

The Hexarchate's technologies depend on consensus mechanics, with the population holding identical beliefs. Heretics who defy its laws and traditions—collectively known as the high calendar—threaten everything from the functioning of FTL stardrives to medical care and power generation. The ritual sacrifice of heretics, a practice demanded by the high calendar, is a small price to pay for the collective good...a price that increasingly troubles you.

But the Hexarchate is at war, and without the great and terrible weapons fueled by those sacrifices, it would lose. As awful as the Hexarchate is, its enemies are worse.

# WHAT THIS GAME IS ABOUT

In Ninefox Gambit RPG, players roleplay hard choices serving the despotic Hexarchate. This can end in three ways: rebellion against the Hexarchate, attempts to reform the system, or assimilation. The rules system is designed to encourage your group to collaborate in exploring your characters' moral dilemmas.

Player characters (PCs) encounter those dilemmas while working in groups toward missions, either in one-shot sessions or longer campaigns. Example missions: defending a military outpost against a heretic attack; investigating the sudden rise of a local politician and their possible ties to heretics; stealing a prototype weapon from a rival faction's lab.

For your convenience, three <u>one-shot adventures</u> by Marie Brennan are included with this game: <u>A Heretical Sacrifice</u> (Rahal and Vidona), <u>Poison from Within</u> (Shuos and Kel), and <u>The Field of Diplomacy</u> (Andan and Nirai).

If you're looking for crunchy space fleet combat, crunchy small-unit tactics, light-hearted hijinks, or uncomplicated heroics, this probably isn't the system for you. These are all fine things! But you'll have better luck finding them in a different system.

(I recommend Starfleet Battles, Pathfinder or D&D or Gloomhaven, Fiasco or Honey Heist, or Tiny Frontiers or Tiny Dungeons, respectively, for these other things!)

I have not included an introduction to RPGs here. This book assumes that you are familiar with tabletop roleplaying games and how they work. If you're new to RPGs, search YouTube for a "Let's Play" for Dungeons & Dragons or FATE or Apocalypse World (or any other popular game you're curious about) for the general idea.

# SETTING NOTE

This game is based on the author's Machineries of Empire series (*Ninefox Gambit*, *Raven Stratagem*, *Revenant Gun*, and *Hexarchate Stories*) but does not require familiarity with the books. While I have included an overview of the baseline setting for your convenience (*see* <u>Appendix B</u>), you should feel free to make *your* Hexarchate unique, to serve your playgroup's needs and interests.

If you *are* familiar with the books, you'll notice that the game mechanics present some of the worldbuilding in altered form, e.g. Vidona do extra physical damage in the game, vs. the "instant death touch" from the books.

If you're here because you've read the books and you want the dirt, keep reading. ;)

# SAFETY AND RELATED CONSIDERATIONS

Ninefox Gambit RPG as written confronts players with upsetting content, such as genocide, atrocity, human sacrifice, imperialism, and complicity in all of the above. As a group, you should make sure that everyone is on board with the version of the Hexarchate you'll be playing in before starting. If you're playing this game, it's probably because you want to engage at some level with themes of imperialism, atrocity, assimilation, and trauma. This implies signing up for a certain amount of discomfort. Still, you should also play in such a way that no one is pushed farther out of their comfort zone *than they want to be*, and players can call a halt to content that bothers them without having to explain themselves.

I recommend using a formal **safety tool** such as one of the following:

John Stavropoulos's **The X-Card**
(https://docs.google.com/document/d/1SB0jsx34bWHZWbnNIVVuMjhDkrdFGo1_hSC2BWPlI3A/edit),

Emily Care Boss's **Lines and Veils**
(https://rpg.stackexchange.com/questions/30906/what-do-the-terms-lines-and-veils-mean),

or Brie Beau Sheldon's **Script Change**
(https://briebeau.com/thoughty/script-change/)

Doing a web search will bring up more information on these tools. At minimum, if anyone needs a time-out from game content at any point, halt the game, make sure they're all right, and edit out the objectionable content before continuing. Call it quits if necessary. **People are more important than games.**

# SPECIAL CONTENT NOTE

If you're thinking of reading the Machineries of Empire books for additional background, please be aware that they include triggers such as suicide and suicidal ideation, gore, child abuse, rape, genocide, imperialism, incest, torture, and more. You should create your own version of the Hexarchate in such a way that it's comfortable for your group. **"Because it's canon" is not a good reason to hurt people.**

# HOW TO PLAY

This game is designed for one Gamemaster (GM) and three to six players.

You'll need a plentiful supply of six-sided dice (d6's) for the GM and each player, writing implements and paper or equivalent, and, optionally, a standard deck of poker cards. A twenty-sided die (d20) may also be helpful for tracking experience points, which can be spent during play for certain benefits.

## GROUP GOAL

Before generating characters, the GM should brief the players on the general shape of the campaign (e.g. a spy mission in enemy territory, rescuing a kidnapped weapons designer). Based on that, all players should agree on a **Group Goal**.

Example Group Goals:

- To expose a corrupt spymaster

- To discover the truth behind the massacre of heretics at the

Battle of Whispered Quartz

- To take over the government of a planet controlled by a rival faction

The goal is determined by the players, not by the plot presented by the GM. The player characters' goal may *subvert* the mission given to them by their employers/higher-ups. For instance, with the first example above, the characters' *orders* may be to "assist the spymaster in penetrating a cabal of heretics," but the *players* may decide that they're going to undermine the spymaster or expose the spymaster's treachery.

# SUMMARY OF CHARACTER CREATION

The kinds of characters who work well in this system are conflicted people. Either they care about doing what's right, but they have compromised themselves in order to survive in a shitty tyranny; or they're loyalists who differ from their leadership on some fundamental points of ethics or policy; or they're people who have committed themselves to the shitty tyranny, but are starting to question their allegiance. The fact that they're conflicted is what makes them vulnerable—and compelling.

IMPORTANT NOTE: This RPG is specifically designed around PCs exploring their moral complicity in a corrupt system. As such, it assumes that all PCs are Hexarchate faction members. For those familiar with the books, non-faction members, foreigners, servitors, and voidmoths are not supported as PCs, although they may appear as NPCs.

1. Pick a **personal name**.

In the Hexarchate, people who join a faction (like the player characters) give up their family names, which are replaced by the faction name. Because the group is more important than the individual, the family/faction name comes first, followed by the personal name.

2. Example: in the name Ajewen Cheris, Ajewen is the family name and Cheris is the personal name. When Cheris joined the Kel faction, the legal name became Kel Cheris.

3. Pick a **faction**. (*See* the list of six available <u>factions</u>. An optional seventh faction, based on the Hexarchate's past history, is detailed in <u>Appendix C</u>.)

4. You'll start at **Rank 1** in your faction.

5. Give your character a **description**. This can include, but need not be limited to, their appearance, pronouns, gender identity, any disabilities and corresponding limitations/accommodations, and so on.

   The Hexarchate is an awful tyranny, but it is welcoming to people of differing sexualities, gender identities, and presentations.

   The most common ethnicity in the Hexarchate resembles East Asians in our world, but you should not feel limited to this. The Hexarchate is an equal-opportunity conqueror.

6. Pick three **Personal Traits**: two **Edges** and one **Heresy**. Select one of the Edges as your **Signifier**. Edges are traits that you can **tag** for extra dice when attempting to accomplish

something; the Edge that is also your Signifier gives you extra experience (XP) when you use it. For example, a character with the Edge *Computers hold no secrets from me* can tag that Edge when attempting to hack a security system. *See* Checks and Tagging.

The Heresy is a belief your character has that sets them at odds with the tyrannical status quo in the Hexarchate.

7. Each character starts with 8 Health. This number may change over time due to injury or subsequent healing, but characters will never have *more* than 8 Health, or less than 0.

# FACTIONS

The Hexarchate is ruled by six factions, each led by a hexarch. With the exception of the Shuos, Hexarchs appoint their successors. There used to be a seventh faction of ethicists, philosophers, and politicians, the Liozh, in the days of the Heptarchate. We do not speak of them. (*See* [Appendix C](#) on the Heptarchate and the Liozh.)

Each PC belongs to one of the Hexarchate's factions. Faction members coordinate with each other both short- and long-term, whether because of specific missions or long-term administration.

Every member of a faction gets their Faction Trait for free. Each character starts as a member of a single faction, with Faction Rank 1, and is therefore complicit in the Hexarchate's tyranny to some degree.

A quick rundown of the factions:

Andan = diplomacy/finance/culture

Kel = military

Nirai = science/technology/medicine

Rahal = legislation/justice

Shuos = spies/assassins/intelligence

Vidona = law enforcement/early education

For example, Kel warships rely on Andan diplomats, Vidona executioners, and Shuos spies; a research facility may be headed by Nirai scientists but depend on Andan financing, Rahal bureaucrats, and Kel security. A strike team that's going after a group of notorious criminals might include Kel or Vidona for muscle, a Nirai hacker, and an Andan or Shuos to serve as the "face."

# ANDAN

Emblem: the kniferose
Motto: *petal-sweet, thorn-sharp*
Colors: blue and silver
Faction Trait: *The way of the rose*
+2d6 when targeting an Edge in combat.

The Andan dominate culture and finance, and are the richest faction. They are also responsible for first contact, diplomacy, and, along with the Vidona, assimilating heretics who are deemed capable of learning to follow the Hexarchate's laws. The Andan value beauty as a weapon, and are more liberal in their use of body-modding than the other factions for utilitarian reasons: to make an impression on others, including foreigners with different aesthetic standards.

**If you're playing an Andan, you're signaling that you're interested in exploring the compromises involved in games of status and social hierarchy.**

What the Andan think of the other factions:

- Kel: A hammer in search of a nail.

- Nirai: Easily manipulated and no threat.

- Rahal: Too wrapped up in the letter of the law to adapt to circumstances as necessity dictates.

- Shuos: Despised rivals competing for influence in the same spheres of interest. The Andan frequently try to outmaneuver the Shuos, whether in business, intelligence, or the court of public opinion. They claim the Shuos were founded by a renegade Andan. (The Shuos claim the reverse.)

- Vidona: An essential tool for maintaining social control. Their blunt methods contrast usefully with the Andan's more subtle ones.

## KEL

Emblem: the ashhawk (also known as "suicide hawk")
Motto: *from every spark a fire*
Colors: black and gold
Faction Trait: *The way of the hawk* +2d6 in physical combat.

The Kel serve as the Hexarchate's military. They are conservative, conformist, and hierarchical. While the Kel have their origins in an independent starfaring nation, some of whose traditions survive today, the average Kel doesn't think about this. These days the Kel are a volunteer army recruiting from anyone who can pass the entrance examinations.

Notably, Kel soldiers are subject to **formation instinct**, brainwashing that makes it difficult for them to disobey orders from a superior officer. **If you're playing a Kel, you're signaling that you're interested in exploring the hard choices involved in the life of a brainwashed soldier.**

What the Kel think of the other factions:

- Andan: The Kel despise the Andan, whom they see as suspect for their cultural flexibility and relations with foreign powers. The average Kel is xenophobic and doesn't see much difference between a foreigner and a heretic.

- Nirai: Strong ties due to Kel dependence on Nirai military innovations.

- Rahal: Kindred souls who share their respect for tradition.

- Shuos: An ambivalent relationship: the Kel and the Shuos often work together, but the Kel are never sure how far they can trust the Shuos, given their reputation for head games.

- Vidona: The Kel grudgingly acknowledge that the Vidona are necessary to preserve the Hexarchate.

## NIRAI

Emblem: the voidmoth
Motto: *every sky is full of stars*
Colors: black and silver
Faction Trait: *The way of the moth*
Once per session, **wind up** or **wind down** the party clock or your personal clock. (*See* Clocks.)

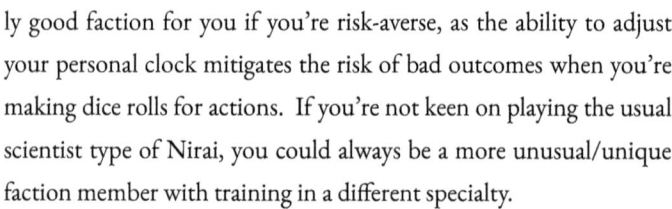

NOTE: Nirai might be an especially good faction for you if you're risk-averse, as the ability to adjust your personal clock mitigates the risk of bad outcomes when you're making dice rolls for actions. If you're not keen on playing the usual scientist type of Nirai, you could always be a more unusual/unique faction member with training in a different specialty.

The Nirai are the faction of mad scientists, engineers, and mathematicians. They're often apolitical, selecting for technical ability rather than ideological purity. Technologies that the Nirai have produced include the mothdrive, which permits faster-than-light (FTL) travel between star systems, and any number of nasty Kel weapons.

**If you're playing a Nirai, you're signaling that you're interested in technology and the questionable ethics involved in its creation or use.**

What the Nirai think of the other factions:

- Andan: Useful for funding research ventures.

- Kel: The Kel's ravenous hunger for new weapons and better starships keeps the Nirai afloat. The average Kel may not be that bright, but it's nice doing business with them.

- Rahal: Rigid and overly concerned with legal niceties.

- Shuos: Overly impressed with their own cleverness. However, the foxes have an insatiable thirst for fancy spy toys, which the Nirai are happy to provide—for a price.

- Vidona: Too similar to the Rahal, but they keep the heretics subdued so Nirai exotic technologies can function. The Nirai maintain close ties to the medical branch of the Vidona.

# RAHAL

Emblem: the scrywolf (also known as "execution wolf")

Motto: *many lenses, one mind*

Colors: gray and bronze

Faction Trait: *The way of the wolf*
+2d6 when investigating someone's Edge.

The Rahal are the Hexarchate's leaders, legislators, and magistrates, responsible for maintaining the high calendar and its regulations. Despite this, their rigid honesty and asceticism mean they are one of the poorer factions. They also protect citizens who have no faction affiliation, who make up the majority of the population. Because local day-cycles on planets or moons require calendrical corrections, they also snap up a certain percentage of the mathematicians.

**If you're playing a Rahal, you're signaling that you're interested in the difficult choices involved in creating or enforcing the Hexarchate's laws.**

What the Rahal think of the other factions:

- Andan: Distressingly xenophilic and flexible in their worldview. However, their diplomats make it possible to deal with foreigners without falling to the corruption of their heretical ideas.

- Kel: A blunt, expendable instrument with which to get the job done.

- Nirai: The Rahal approve of the Nirai as the two factions are invested in the mathematics of the state religion.

- Shuos: Unreliable, not least because of their habit of producing unstable geniuses. One of the Hexarchate's greatest liabilities, if only the intelligence they provide weren't so useful.

- Vidona: Nobody likes them, but their work policing the Hexarchate is necessary. The Rahal accord them a certain grudging respect.

## SHUOS

Emblem: the ninefox (also known as "eyefox")

Motto: *the more eyes the better*

Colors: red and gold

Faction Trait: *The way of the fox*

+2d6 when attempting to deceive someone or something.

The Shuos are strategists responsible for intelligence operations and are known for their cunning, amorality, and love of games. They would be more feared for their assassins and spies if not for their extreme instability. Unlike the other factions, Shuos tradition is for their Hexarch to claim the seat by assassination. A good Shuos Hexarch is lucky to last a decade.

**If you're playing a Shuos, you're signaling that you're interested in exploring the dubious ethics involved when it comes to playing games with other people's lives.**

What the Shuos think of the other factions:

- Andan: The Shuos hate the Andan. Not only are the Andan richer (the Shuos are usually juggling budget shortfalls), the general populace likes them better. Also, Andan specialties overlap with those of the Shuos, and the competitive Shuos find this infuriating.

- Kel: The Shuos work closely with the Kel in a military context, although their view of the Kel is condescending: "Distract the enemy with guns so we can get the real work done."

- Nirai: Necessary, but frequently naive about the implications of their research.

- Rahal: The Shuos tolerate the Rahal's leadership, but only just, and enjoy testing their authority.

- Vidona: A blunt instrument that damages the Hexarchate in the long term.

# **VIDONA**

Emblem: the stingray
Motto: *through blood we prevail*
Colors: green and bronze
Faction Trait: *The way of the stingray*

+2 damage in unarmed combat.

The Vidona enforce the Hexarchate's laws and sacrifice heretics on remembrance days. A few are doctors specializing in keeping heretics alive for their intended purpose. The Vidona are also responsible for education (read: indoctrination) up to the age of seventeen (the age of majority in the Hexarchate). The rest of the Hexarchate reviles them, and they are more insular and conservative than the other factions.

**If you're playing a Vidona, you're signaling that you're interested in exploring the terrible choices that come up when you're responsible for enforcing the Hexarchate's sacrifices and rules.**

What the Vidona think of the other factions:

- Andan: The Andan's squabbling with the Shuos is disloyal and should not be tolerated.

- Kel: Admirable loyalty. The Hexarchate's necessary fist.

- Nirai: The Vidona maintain close ties to the medical branch of the Nirai, although their emphases differ.

- Rahal: The architects of the system. The Vidona have great respect for them.

- Shuos: The Shuos's squabbling with the Andan is disloyal and should not be tolerated.

# PERSONAL TRAITS

## PERSONAL TRAITS: EDGES

Your character starts with two **Edges**. These represent your character's advantages. In general, your character has a number of Edges equal to their Faction Rank +1.

Each Edge starts with 8 points. Edge points may change over time, from a minimum of 0 to a maximum of 8. When an Edge reaches 0 points, it is **knocked out** and cannot be tagged for extra dice until it is restored.

You'll want to make sure that your Edges will come up often enough to be useful during play! An Edge like *I am a veteran soldier* can be invoked in more situations than *I am great with daggers*. For example characters and their Edges, *see* Appendix D.

## PERSONAL TRAITS: HERESY

Your character's Heresy is the central moral dilemma that haunts them. It's something that could cause your character to defy the Hexarchate. A Heresy can never be removed.

## PERSONAL TRAITS: COMPLICATIONS

During the course of play, your character may gain **Complications**, which are other challenges your characters may face. Complications do not have points associated with them, only Edges do. Your character gains a Complication every time an Edge is knocked out. The player can remove a Complication during Character Advancement if they meet the requirements.

*See* Appendix D for example characters and their Edges, Heresies, and Complications.

## SIGNIFIERS

One of your Edges is your **Signifier**. This is a publicly known Personal Trait that indicates a core part of your character's identity. In the Hexarchate, the shape of your shadow reflects your Signifier. It's up to the player to come up with a shadow that feels right for their Signifier.

For example, if your Signifier is *I impress people with my beauty and bearing*, your shadow might be *a magnificent peacock*. A character whose Signifier is *My strength is like the dignity of an ancient tree* might have, as their shadow, *an unbowed pine*.

## ON DISABILITY AND PERSONAL TRAITS

You are welcome to create disabled characters! The disability (or disabilities) can simply be declared as part of your character's identity like their gender or hair color, as well as associated limitations and any technological accommodations you wish for your character to have (e.g. hearing aids for deafness, wheelchair for mobility). If you wish to play a character whose disability is a challenge for them, you may optionally make it an additional Complication. Feel free to use multiple Complications to represent multiple disabilities. You should discuss with the GM whether these disabilities are curable or incurable; incurable disabilities should not be removed as Complications.

If a disability is *not* a Complication, it should not be played as a source of difficulty for that character.

# LOCATION TRAITS

The Hexarchate starts with the following two **Location Traits**, which can be tagged at any time within its borders.

*Loyalty to the Hexarchate is the highest virtue.*
*The lesser must submit to the will of the greater.*

Specific locations may also have Location Traits reflecting local conditions. These can also be tagged when characters are on-site. For example:

*It's always rainy in the Marsh of Drowned Souls.*
*Music is highly esteemed in the City of Kaleidoscope Joys.*
*A black hole guards the approach to the Fortress of Stifled Paths.*

Location Traits have 8 points, and can be targeted and knocked out like characters' Edges (*see* Edge Combat). Once a Location Trait is knocked out, it cannot be tagged anymore.

As an optional rule, players and the GM may also tag **Calendrical Traits** pertaining to the specific day and the Hexarchate's religious observances. See Appendix A.

# CLOCKS

There are three kinds of clocks: your **Personal Clock**, the **Party Clock**, and the **Hexarchate Clock**.

## PERSONAL CLOCK

Your **Personal Clock** starts at 1 and has a minimum of 1. This means that when you roll a check, any 1's are successes. If your Personal Clock is at 3, then 1's, 2's, and 3's are successes, and so on.

If your Personal Clock ever reaches 6 or above, you have been **Assimilated** and control of your character passes to the GM. The player creates a new character at the same rank as the old one. If two characters in the party have been Assimilated during the course of the campaign, the game ends.

## PARTY CLOCK

The **Party Clock** starts at 1 and has a minimum of 1. This means that when two or more party members cooperate on a check, any 1's are successes. If the Party Clock is a 4, then 1's, 2's, 3's, and 4's are successes, and so on.

If the Party Clock ever reaches 6 or above, the party has been Assimilated and the game ends.

Managing Personal and Party Clocks will be a balancing act. You may want to leave a Clock wound up in order to make it easier to succeed on checks, because you'll get more successes. On the other hand, you may want to wind down a Clock to avoid being Assimilated.

## HEXARCHATE CLOCK

The **Hexarchate Clock** is different from the other two clocks. It starts at 6. If the Hexarchate Clock ever reaches 12 or above, the party has been Assimilated and the game ends.

If the Hexarchate Clock ever reaches 0 or below, the Hexarchate has been overthrown or mass rebellion erupts, and the game ends. Alternately, if your group prefers, you can continue your campaign, perhaps by exploring the question of what happens next.

OPTIONAL: For a larger campaign, you may also include **Region Clocks** to represent areas smaller than the entire Hexarchate or places that are home to potential rebellions. A Region Clock starts at 6. If it ever reaches 12 or above, the region is Assimilated. If it reaches 0 or below, it rebels against the Hexarchate.

At various points you will **wind up** or **wind down** the value of a clock. To wind up a clock, add 1 to its value. To wind down a clock, subtract 1 from its value.

You may **wind down** your Personal Clock **at any time** by spending 1 XP. The Party Clock can be wound down for 4 XP and the Hexarchate Clock can also be wound down for 60 XP, but **only at the end of a session**. (See Advancement.)

# CHECKS AND TAGGING

In general, gameplay should only require characters to roll Checks when an Edge or Signifier is involved, or when an action would advance the party's Goal. Otherwise, players are free to express their characters' side actions through narration without rolling a Check that might additionally run the risk of rolling a 6 (*see* Rolling 6's, below).

## INDIVIDUAL CHECKS

Base: roll 3d6. If your Personal Clock is 1, then any 1's are successes. If it is 2, then any 1's or 2's are successes, and so on.

Gain +1d6 (Edge) for each non-Signifier Edge of yours that you tag, explaining how it applies to the situation. A given Edge can be tagged only once per test.
Gain +2d6 (Signifier) if you tag your Signifier.
Gain +1d6 for each Location Trait that you tag.

Gain +1d6 if you tag the Edge of a friendly NPC. Each NPC can only help once per test in this manner.

OPTIONAL: Gain +1d6 if you tag the Calendrical Trait for the day (see [Appendix A](#)).

The GM's word is final as to whether a given tag makes sense, or a given NPC is friendly or not, for a specific check. Be persuasive!

The more successes you roll, the more impressive your action.

One to two successes mean that you have succeeded, at a cost (situational) that makes progress more difficult. You should narrate what happens, including the cost.

Three to five successes mean that you have easily carried out your action. You should narrate what happens.

Six or more successes mean that you have carried out an astonishing feat. You should narrate what happens.

If you do not roll any successes, then the action fails and the GM narrates what happens.

Example: You're trying to persuade a guard to let you inspect a Rahal magistrate's office.

- If you rolled one or two successes, the guard might demand that you fetch them a rare but highly fashionable pet that their daughter covets.

- If you rolled three to five successes, the guard stands aside and lets you in.

- If you rolled six or more successes, the guard not only lets you in, but helps cover up all evidence that you were ever there, and might also be an ally in the future.

- If you didn't roll any successes, the guard raises the alarm and reinforcements come pouring in.

If you succeed at your action, and you tagged your Signifier, **mark 1 Experience (1 XP)**. (Tagging a regular Edge doesn't grant XP, only the Signifier.)

If you succeed at your action, and it advanced the Party Goal, **mark 1 XP**. The GM's judgment is final as to whether the Party Goal has been advanced.

If you confronted or revealed your Heresy, regardless of whether the action succeeded, **mark 3 XP**.

## ROLLING 6's

If you succeed at your action, and you rolled any 6's, then you must also **wind up** either your Personal Clock, the Group Clock, or the Hexarchate Clock.

A 6 is always a **failure**, even for an Assimilated character (e.g. an Assimilated NPC).

Note: If your PC's Personal Clock is at 5 and it's wound up, you may immediately spend banked XP to keep from being Assimilated.

## GROUP CHECK

A Group Check works like an Individual Check, with a base roll of 3d6, except you use the Party Clock to determine successes instead. You should designate a single person to make the die roll for the group. The Edges of any PC involved can be tagged for dice. The characters involved in the Group Check should decide together what the result of any success is.

As with individual checks, the GM's word is final as to whether a given tag makes sense, or a given NPC is friendly or not, for a specific check. Be persuasive!

If the group succeeds at the action, any participant who tagged their Signifier **marks 1 XP**.

In addition, if the action advanced the Party Goal, anyone who participated **marks 1 XP**.

Any participant who confronted or revealed their Heresy, regardless of whether the action succeeded, **marks 3 XP**.

If the Group Check succeeds, and you rolled any 6's, then you must also **wind up** the Personal Clock of one of the people involved (this should be a volunteer), the Group Clock, or the Hexarchate Clock.

## OPPOSED CHECK

An Opposed Check works similarly to a regular check, except two opposed parties (either PCs or NPCs) roll, each starting with a base 3d6. Each party may tag their own Edges if applicable. In an opposed check, you may additionally gain 1d6 for tagging an opponent's Complication and explaining how it applies to the situation. Each Complication can be tagged once per test. The person who has the most successes prevails. The greater the margin of successes the winner rolls over the loser, the more significant their victory. For example, if the winner rolled 9 successes and the loser rolled 5 successes, the margin is 4 successes and the winner easily carries out their action.

If the winner is a player character and they rolled any 6's in their check, they must **wind up** their Personal Clock, the Group Clock, or the Hexarchate Clock.

Example:

Rahal Jayna is in a small, dark room questioning Ae to figure out if Ae, an eyewitness to a murder, is lying to her. Jayna rolls a base 3d6, plus 2d6 for tagging her own Signifier Edge *I have a keen nose for deception* and an additional 1d6 for tagging Ae's Complication *My face is an open book*. Ae also has the Complication *I'm a terrible shuttle pilot*, but Jayna can't tag it in this situation because it's not relevant to the action.

For their part, Ae rolls a base 3d6, plus 1d6 for tagging their Trait *I don't bow to authority* and an additional 1d6 for tagging Jayna's Complication *I have claustrophobia*, which makes it harder for Jayna to concentrate in such a confined space. Ae can't tag Jayna's Complication *I have a horrible relationship with my parents* here, as Jayna's parents are on the other side of the galaxy and not available for intervention (much to Jayna's relief).

# COMBAT

In the Hexarchate, the authorities require little excuse to commit violence against heretics. Non-heretical crime against ordinary citizens is usually dealt with by mediation/community service (traffic tickets or petty theft), brainwashing (violent crime or embezzling), or execution (murder or treason), depending on the severity of the offense. Conveniently, "treason" is often reclassified as a heresy.

Crime committed by faction members is usually punished by the faction's own authorities. Notably, assassination is a normal way to advance rank in the Shuos faction, so a *successful* assassination is usually not punished. The rest of the Hexarchate usually leaves them alone as long as the collateral damage isn't too bad (or the bribes are good).

**Heresy** can range from minor infractions that citizens escape with a slap on the wrist and a fine, medium infractions that result in stepped-up surveillance (the Hexarchate is a surveillance state and keeps track of its citizens' "loyalty") or remedial brainwashing, to major infractions for which the luckless heretic can be executed or sacrificed.

Minor infractions include being late to or missing the occasional remembrance or showing open disrespect to faction officials carrying out their duties.

Medium infractions include continuously missing remembrances or unauthorized possession of heretical books or materials.

Major infractions include actively promoting or living by a heretical calendar or religion, helping heretics escape or freeing them outright, or attacking faction officials carrying out their religious duties.

**Combat** takes place between individuals and is abstract.

## PHYSICAL COMBAT

**Physical combat** is an opposed roll. The winner of the roll deals 2 damage to the loser's Health. (Everyone starts at 8 Health when fully healed.) The loser may optionally take some or all damage to an Edge or Edges of their choice instead, distributing it as desired. On a tie, both sides take 1 damage.

However, if an Edge is **knocked out** (reduced to 0), it cannot be tagged until it is restored above 0. Gain a new Complication. The person dealing the damage decides on the Complication, which should make sense for the situation.

When you reach 0 Health, you are unconscious or incapacitated. Gain a Complication. The person dealing the damage decides on the Complication. Your Health cannot be reduced below 0.

Combat ends when one side flees, surrenders, or cannot fight anymore. Keep in mind that heretics in particular have a strong incentive not to surrender unless they're truly screwed, because they're going to be sacrificed anyway. Fleeing, where possible, is much more likely. The

Hexarchate is powerful—but it's a big galaxy, and help for heretics and rebels exists in unlikely places.

Example: Jedao takes 2 damage from a Kel duelist. He can distribute 1 damage to Health and 1 damage to Edge: *I'm good at reading people*, or 1 damage to Edge: *I always have a plan* and 1 damage to Edge: *I'm good at reading people*, or 2 damage to Edge: *I'm good at reading people*, and so on.

If Jedao went down to 0 Health in the fight, the Kel duelist can inflict the Complication *I am a coward who flees from physical confrontation* or *I am missing a leg* or *I have a disfiguring scar that causes people to flinch from me*. On the other hand, the Complication *I am disastrous at baking* doesn't make sense here.

(*See* below under Edge combat for an example of a knocked-out Edge and Complications.)

## EDGE COMBAT

**Edge combat** is an opposed roll targeting an Edge that is either known or has been guessed. (The signifier is automatically known.). If the person initiating combat wins the roll, and they know or **successfully** guessed the Edge, they deal 2 damage to that Edge. If they tie the roll, and they know or successfully guessed the Edge, they deal 1 damage to that Edge. If they lose the roll or guess incorrectly, the target may react negatively, but no damage is dealt. It's the GM's call as to whether a guess is "close enough for government work."

If an Edge is **knocked out** (reduced to 0), it cannot be tagged until it is restored above 0. Gain a new Complication. The person dealing the damage decides what the Complication is.

Edges cannot be reduced below 0.

Example: A Nirai saboteur knocks out Nirai Kujen's Edge *I have mastered the eldritch sciences of the Hexarchate.* The saboteur could inflict the Complication *I am too rattled by recent misfortunes to concentrate* or *Recent scientific advances have rendered my knowledge obsolete*. On the other hand, *I am having a crisis of conscience over my inventions* is hard to justify because it directly contradicts a preexisting Complication, *I no longer understand the chains of conscience.* (It would be a different matter if Kujen had previously bought off the latter Complication—in which case you could justify it as character development!)

# HEALING AND RECOVERY

Inevitably, your characters will sustain damage to their Edges and/or Health, and want to recover.

To **recover** 4 points of Edge and/or Health damage (to be distributed as you wish), play out your Heresy or one of your Complications in a way at least one other player character can witness or be involved in. The more the merrier!

Example: A Vidona propagandist's Heresy is her objection to human sacrifice—her belief in the system has been shaken by seeing the human cost up-close while touring a heretic processing facility. She uses her influence to smuggle a heretic prisoner to safety, but another character catches her at it and argues with her because of the risk of being caught and punished by the authorities.

# MONEY AND RESOURCES

As a faction member, you are able to draw upon the faction's resources when doing sanctioned work (or pretending to). This doesn't mean that you're strictly limited to the resources appropriate to your rank, if you or your group is either very persuasive or devises a scheme to coax additional resources out of the people who control them.

You should not have to track "gold" or keep a spreadsheet of expenses in this game. Rank is an approximate gauge of the kind of responsibility you have as well as the resources you are able to access. If there's any question as to whether a resource is reasonable or not, the GM's word is final.

Rank 1

You are responsible for yourself.

Rank 2

You are responsible for an organization of around 10 people.

Rank 3

You are responsible for an organization of around 50 people.

<u>Rank 4</u>
You are responsible for an organization of around 100 people.

<u>Rank 5</u>
You are responsible for an organization of around 500 people.

<u>Rank 6</u>
This rank is reserved for NPCs. At this rank, you are a Hexarch. You are responsible for the entire faction and have full access to any of its resources, and possibly beyond, at the cost of being inextricably enmeshed with the Hexarchate's crimes.

# ADVANCEMENT

t any time, you may spend Experience (XP) as follows:

<u>1 XP</u>

- wind down your Personal Clock

You also may do this immediately to keep from being Assimilated if your Personal Clock is at 5 and it gets wound up.

**At the end of the session**, you may spend Experience (XP) as follows:

<u>4 XP</u>

- change an Edge, with the GM's permission

- change your Signifier to a different Edge

- wind down someone else's Personal Clock, with their permission

- wind down the Party Clock. **Special:** Multiple players may pool their XP to pay for this.

## 12 XP

- gain a rank in your faction. Each time you gain a rank, gain an Edge as well.

- remove a Complication, with the GM's permission

## 60 XP

- wind down the Hexarchate Clock

**Special:** Multiple players may pool their XP to pay for this.

# GUIDE TO GAMING

This is not a general guide to GMing; as aforementioned, Ninefox Gambit RPG assumes that you're familiar with how TTRPGs (tabletop roleplaying games) work. That said, this game does have some challenges that are specific to this setting and these rules, as discussed below.

## Safety.

This was mentioned at the beginning of the book, but it's important enough to mention again here. Because the Hexarchate and this game deal with potentially upsetting material, it's your responsibility as the GM to set the tone, make sure that your players are comfortable with the version of the Hexarchate that you're playing in together, and that everyone continues to feel safe throughout play.

## Setting the party up for success.

This game was designed with the intention that the party is a group of comrades who work together toward a common goal of their choice based on the initial adventure hook that you provide them. If any players seem inclined to design a character who doesn't fit into this framework, you'll have to intervene. If a player *really* wants to play the Lone Asshole Who Refuses To Work With the Party (or worse, *is* the Lone Asshole in real life), boot them. I can't say it plainer than that. The game will only be as successful as the group's chemistry is. (*See* also Assimilation vs. Rebellion, below.)

## Setting individual characters up for success.

Some players may ask for help or need nudging to create characters that work well in this game. The core of this game is centered around **messy, conflicted characters who are pushed by atrocity until either they are broken or they break an oppressive system**. I've bolded that because it's important, and you should feel free to say it to any players who are having difficulty solidifying a character concept.

In particular, it's helpful to vet characters' Edges to make sure they are things that can reasonably come up during play as advantages, and their Heresies to make sure they will provide the conflicts that drive play forward. For example, an Edge like *People find me charming* or *I have quick reflexes* may have more general applicability than a narrower Edge like *I am a master of flower-arranging*, depending on your campaign. You may find it helpful to refer players to Appendix D, with its example NPC characters, for inspiration.

If a player is struggling here, be supportive and help them brainstorm—the point is not to penalize them, but to assist them in coming up with a character that will be rewarding to play.

Players may discover during the first few sessions of the game that there's a disparity between the character they *thought* would be enjoyable to play and what they *really* want to play. In cases like these, I advise allowing them to revise their characters (e.g. changing their Edges, Signifier, and/or Heresy) without XP cost or penalty.

## Character Death.

You'll have noticed that PCs are *not* killed when they go to 0 Health, but are simply knocked out. This is because **the biggest threat in this game is not death, but Assimilation**. In this game, this means that you have become so thoroughly enmeshed with the Hexarchate's tyranny and hegemony that you cannot separate yourself from it. This isn't to say that PCs can't die, but they should only die if their players decide it should happen narratively. In the case of character death, the player should be welcome to create another character at the same Rank if they want to keep playing. Adopting a friendly NPC might be one way to handle this.

## Assimilation vs. Rebellion.

You'll probably get a sense early on whether individual characters or the party as a whole is leaning in one direction or another. Play up the conflict—which is the core of the game—while giving players an opportunity to explore the dilemmas that are most interesting to them. If the party is determined to take down the Hexarchate or die trying, craft your adventures accordingly.

One caution: while it may be viable for the *characters* to have differing opinions on assimilation vs. rebellion, this has the potential to blow up if the *players* are split down the middle on this. Consider having a "Session Zero" in which players come to a working agreement on their approach.

## Npcs.

NPCs (non-player characters) are similar to PCs, except non-faction NPCs will not have a Faction Trait, and they do not necessarily have a Heresy. NPCs have a Signifier for XP-gaining purposes. Rank for non-faction NPCs simply determines how many Edges they have (Rank + 1). This includes Hexarchate citizens who are not faction members, foreigners, aliens (including voidmoths), and servitors or other AIs. *See* Appendix D for some examples.

For NPCs, their Personal Clock acts strictly as a measure of possible success (for example, an NPC with a Personal Clock of 3 succeeds on 1's, 2's, and 3's). NPCs do not usually wind up or wind down Clocks. Exception: Nirai NPCs, like PCs, can wind a clock up or down once per session. It's up to the GM whether they wish to allow PCs to likewise allow Nirai PCs to adjust NPCs' clocks.

Special note: for Assimilated characters, treat their Personal Clock as 5 (not 6) for purposes of determining successes on rolls. In other words, **a roll of 6 is always a failure**.

## Setting.

The Hexarchate as written is high-technology, low-realism magitech space opera: think Star Trek or Star Wars rather than *The Expanse*. Space is "friendly," FTL (faster-than-light) travel is easy, relativistic effects are ignored, and tech is such that most planets are either terraformed or relatively easy to survive on. That said, there's no reason why *your* Hexarchate couldn't be on the more realistic/deadly end of the scale. Just be sure to communicate this to your players beforehand so they're not taken by surprise!

## Items.

Just as with the setting, the default assumption is that high-tech handwavium-powered science fantasy items are readily available: personal blasters, force swords, easy medical care/healing and accommodations. Feel free to use your imagination, or to solicit ideas from your players! If they want a space opera gewgaw, let them have it (perhaps with a cost). You'll notice that physical combat involves flat damage that doesn't change with weapon type. That's deliberate; the philosophy of this game is that any weapon (even an improvised one) is deadly in the hand of a trained wielder. The focus of this game is not exhaustive, "realistic" combat simulation but the exploration of moral dilemmas.

## Mass combat and space battles.

This is a space opera setting, so inevitably someone is going to be interested in space battles. The focus should always be on the PCs as the heroes of whatever action is happening, rather than the machinations of distant admirals. This rules set is not optimized to provide a granular simulation of single-ship combat (e.g. Artemis: Starship Bridge Simulator or Starfinder) or fleet battles (e.g. Star Fleet Battles). Keep your space battles narratively focused on the PCs and their actions, and you'll be fine.

# SAMPLE CHARACTER SHEET

Name:
 Faction:
Rank:
Description

TRAITS
Faction Trait

Edge (8)

Edge (8)

Heresy

Complications

Health (8)

Personal Clock (1)
Party Clock (1)

Experience

# EXAMPLE CHARACTER

NOTE: Appendix D additionally includes the following sample Rank 1 characters (one for each faction): Andan Eri, Kel Tarun, Liozh Votta, Nirai Areth, Rahal Mistrikor, Shuos Yeren, and Vidona Elpen. There are also examples of higher-Rank characters.

Name: Andan Kiruet
Faction: Andan
Rank: 1

Description: Kiruet is a short, elegant person with curly blue hair. Zie compensates for zir deafness with advanced hearing aids.

TRAITS
Faction Trait: *The way of the rose*
+2d6 when targeting an Edge in combat.

Edge (8)
*I have family connections in unexpected places.*
SIGNIFIER: *a tangle of grape vines*

Edge (8)
*I have a keen eye for discrepancies.*

Heresy
*I don't believe that heretics deserve to die.*

Health (8)

Personal Clock: 1
Party Clock: 1

# ONE-SHOT ADVENTURES

## INTRODUCTION

The three adventure scenarios below are each designed for a specific pair of factions, exemplifying two alternate approaches to dealing with the problem. Neither the factions nor the approaches should be taken as a straitjacket: you can run these adventures with other kinds of characters and other types of approaches. You are also welcome to alter details about the NPCs, such as their gender, if desired.

That having been said, each adventure is particularly tailored to the concerns of the factions listed, e.g. Rahal and Vidona for a plot involving heretics and the maintenance of the high calendar. The included approaches also cater to the typical strengths of those factions. Running the Andan/Nirai adventure about contact with a foreign emissary (which is tailored to be solved with diplomacy or stealth) for a pack of xenophobic Kel might require the GM to make some adjustments!

The writeup for each adventure is broken into several sections. The *Overview* is designed to give the GM context for the plot and a broad summary of its central conflict. The next three sections break the adventure into three acts: the *Setup* introduces the problem, the *Development* introduces complications, and the *Crisis* puts the PCs to a difficult choice, asking how they will resolve the issue. The options presented there are not exhaustive; if the players come up with a plausible alternative solution, by all means let them pursue it! But remember, the world of the *Ninefox Gambit RPG* is not one that lends itself to clean and heroic victories: doing the morally right thing often comes with a cost, not just to the PCs but to the ordinary citizens of the Hexarchate.

Where there is **boldface text** within the adventure, this signals a task that could require a check. These particularly come up in instances where the task is opposed by an NPC. However, the GM has a great deal of flexibility around requiring checks: since each one has a chance of advancing a PC or Party Clock, a higher frequency of rolls can make the game more perilous. Calling for many checks is appropriate if you are fleshing the adventure out into a larger experience played across multiple sessions, perhaps constituting the entirety of a short campaign. If, however, the adventure is being used as part of a longer-term campaign, limiting the number of checks may be necessary to avoid pushing the PCs too rapidly toward Assimilation.

Each adventure also includes a *Variations* section, which offers thoughts on how to raise the grimness and horror to the level seen in the Machineries of Empire series and how to play out longer-term consequences if the adventure is used in a larger campaign. Following this, there are character sheets for major NPCs and four pre-generated

PCs tailored to the adventure. (If not using the pre-gens, you may wish to discuss the nature of the plot with the players in advance, to avoid ending up with characters whose Edges and Heresies are ill-suited to the circumstances.)

The assumption here is that the PCs are Rank 1; however, you can run these adventures with more advanced characters. If you do so, simply adjust the NPCs to be one or two ranks higher than the PCs, so as to provide a continuing challenge.

# 1. A HERETICAL SACRIFICE

**Factions:** Rahal, Vidona
**Approaches:** diplomacy, combat

This adventure, the most orthodox of the three, is designed to make the players confront the challenge of achieving even small-scale change for the better within a hostile system.

## Overview

Thanks to a localized heresy and the efforts of an overzealous Kel general, the primary moon of the planet Qaluj, Gayare, has been bombed into uninhabitable rubble. Both the heresy and the loss of the population there have destabilized the local calendrical gradient. In order to fix this, Rahal Arax, Senior Magistrate of Hreng, Qaluj's secondary moon, has been tasked with supplying a dozen heretics for a sacrifice on the surface of Gayare, which will restore the calendar's effects.

Unfortunately for the people of Hreng, Arax is running short on heretics. Hreng has always been a model society, and any traces of disobedience among the locals have been suppressed for the time being by the fate of Gayare. Since Arax is unwilling to admit to his superiors that he cannot supply the necessary victims, he has arrested a dozen loyal citizens, secretly ditching what passes for due process in the Hexarchate in order to label them heretics suitable for sacrifice.

The PCs are assigned to transport the prisoners to Gayare and perform the sacrifice there. If they are obedient cogs in the machine, this will go off without a hitch. If they pay attention to the discrepancies, however, they will soon realize that Arax has shredded even the thin semblance of the promise the Hexarchate makes to its citizens: that if they are loyal and obedient, then they will be safe.

Will the PCs carry out their duties as ordered? Or will they take action to rescue the innocent victims—knowing that by doing so, they endanger the stability of the high calendar in the area?

## Setup

When the PCs arrive on Hreng to collect the heretics, Arax provides them as usual with a script to recite for the camera while performing the sacrifice. Such scripts are formulaic, but this one is peculiarly thin on details regarding the victims' heresy, speaking only in generic terms of their "crimes against the Hexarchate." (Arax is not imaginative enough to create anything interesting.)

He also says something odd, which is that he has placed locked gags on the victims to prevent them from talking. **If pressed as to why,** he claims they have some kind of exotic technology or perhaps nascent faction-style ability that makes their words unnaturally persuasive; if the PCs question this remarkable claim, he says that the need to sacrifice them as soon as possible has prevented him from investigating further. He then orders the PCs to get underway and delay him no further with questions.

Anyone who studied Arax's shadow notes that it takes the shape of a twisting, writhing eel. **Inquiry into his background** suggests that it is an ambush eel, an aquatic predator from his home planet of Emni; they camouflage themselves to resemble their surroundings and are very difficult to catch. They have a negative reputation on Emni as deceitful, untrustworthy creatures.

The PCs have very little time to spend investigating if they are to arrive on Gayare and perform the sacrifice on schedule; delaying is tantamount to open insubordination. Furthermore, Arax has taken steps to block discovery. Any attempt **to query the grid** about the background of the twelve heretics turns up nothing: their personal records have been wiped. While this is not unusual procedure for the Rahal (the Hexarchate likes to erase heretics from its history, unless they need to be used as especially gruesome object lessons), it *is* unusual—borderline insubordinate—for Arax to have done this prior to the remembrance.

It is possible, however, to discover where the heretics came from. They were all part of a mining community that shows no particular signs of heresy either in the past or at present. Formerly a minority population called the Khamde, they have abandoned their low language in favor of the Hexarchate's high language and lost most of their distinctive traditions. The only one that survives in any strength is one useful in the often-noisy mines: a native sign language.

## Development

Assuming the PCs do not openly defy Arax at the outset, they will board a small moth headed to Gayare. A small squadron of Vidona accompanies them, under the command of Vidona Dzon, in case any other heretics attempt to intervene and rescue the prisoners. Here, too, the PCs' time is limited: the flight to Gayare is not a long one.

When the prisoners are brought on board, the oldest of the heretics, a man named Pothiset, begins moving his hands in ways that suggest a form of communication. This can be identified as Khamde sign language and translated **with the help of the grid**. Dzon, the only person other than Rahal Arax who knows the full and true story, moves swiftly to beat Pothiset down. She then binds not only his hands, but those of all the heretics, passing it off as a security measure.

The gags cannot be removed without **a great deal of effort** (which would also ruin them for future use), but if the PCs approach Pothiset **away from Dzon** and give him the opportunity to converse with his hands, he protests tearfully that he and his group are not heretics; they are loyal citizens who were taken from their beds without justification. Everything he says corroborates the hints the PCs may have picked up on before about Arax's improper behavior.

GMs who wish to give their players a second chance in the event of this first one failing may also include a stowaway aboard the moth, a young alt of the former Khamde named Riyothai. They, still having their tongue, likewise share the story of the prisoners' innocence. Riyothai is so desperate for Pothiset and the others to be saved, they offer their own life in exchange. Unfortunately for Riyothai, the sacrifice requires a full twelve victims: to kill just one will do no good at all.

## Crisis

Before or just after arriving at Gayare, the PCs must decide what to do with the information they have received. If they carry out the sacrifice as ordered, either through ignorance of the true situation or obedience to their orders, afterward a trio of people from the mining population commit public suicide in protest of the unjust execution, setting off a minor wave of heresy on Hreng that is crushed without mercy.

If the PCs wish to prevent the unjust sacrifice, they may contact the Rahal bureaucracy and report Arax's misbehavior. This creates **a diplomatic struggle** in which they must present the evidence they have gathered and contest Arax's own report to persuade their superior that the Senior Magistrate is in the wrong. If they succeed, a quick discussion between the Rahal and the Vidona results in a last-second order to stand down from the remembrance, saving the lives of Pothiset and his people.

Alternatively, the PCs—perhaps fearing, quite justifiably, that any such report will not be resolved in time to do any good—may choose to prioritize saving the innocent, and deal with the consequences later. If they balk at performing the sacrifice, without first having set in motion the diplomatic machinery, this leads to a **violent confrontation** with Vidona Dzon and her squadron. She is determined to protect the calendar, whatever the cost, and will kill the prisoners by any means she can even if the remembrance cannot be carried out as it should be. The Vidona group should be equal in number to the party, with all except Dzon at the same Rank as the PCs.

It is even possible that the PCs may choose to leap straight into open rebellion at some point along the way, e.g. by **hijacking the ship** before it reaches Gayare and fleeing with the imprisoned miners.

Such drastic action is likely to have significant consequences, but that doesn't mean the players won't opt for it!

Whatever route the players choose, failing to perform the sacrifice has negative effects for the local calendrical gradient. The technology that maintains atmospheric conditions for agriculture on Hreng becomes unreliable, resulting in a local famine.

The GM may also choose to have these outcomes affect the Hexarchate Clock. Upholding the sacrifices winds it up it by one step; exposing Arax's corruption or openly rebelling against performing the sacrifice can wind it down one step.

## Variations

In place of the generic "sacrifice" described above, you may substitute the more specific Remembrance of Interlaced Hands. This ritual involves peeling the skin back from the hands of the heretics, then using the still-attached strips to bind them together in a circle.

Similarly, both Rahal Arax and Vidona Dzon can take more brutal measures to prevent the prisoners from talking: Arax by removing the victims' tongues instead of gagging them, and Dzon by breaking the hands of Pothiset and the rest of his compatriots. The miners who protest the sacrifice commit suicide by public immolation, i.e. setting themselves on fire.

If the PCs move to prevent the sacrifice, either through diplomacy or combat, they may make a long-term enemy of Arax and his supporters within the bureaucracy, Dzon and her supporters within the police, or both. This enmity can manifest as anything from hostility within the faction that denies the PCs supplies and support to charges of heresy leveled against them.

# NPCS

**Rahal Arax** (he/him)

*Rank:* 2

*Clock:* 2

*Faction Trait:* the way of the wolf (+2d6 when investigating someone's Edge)

*Signifier Edge:* I'm an expert at bending systems to my bidding.

*Signifier:* a twisting, writhing eel

*Edges:* I know the Hexarchate bureaucracy inside and out.

I control my sphere of power with an iron fist.

*Complications:* I lack imagination.

I have failed up to the level of my incompetence.


**Vidona Dzon** (she/her)

*Rank:* 2

*Clock:* 2

*Faction Trait:* the way of the stingray (+2 damage in unarmed combat)

*Signifier Edge:* I will do whatever the Hexarchate requires.

*Signifier:* stingrays swimming in formation

*Edges:* My control of my region is absolute.

I am a living encyclopedia of laws.

*Complication:*

I've been chastised for too frequently solving problems by killing.


**Generic Vidona Muscle**

*Rank:* 1

*Clock:* 2

*Faction Trait:* the way of the stingray (+2 damage in unarmed combat)

*Edge:* I do not hesitate to crush the enemies of the Hexarchate.

**Pothiset** (he/him)

*Rank:* Non-faction

*Clock:* 1

*Signifier Edge:* As a community elder, I take care of my people.

*Signifier:* flashes of light in a scattering of gravel

*Edge:* I can forge a meaningful connection with almost anyone.

*Complication:* I've been accused of heresy by Rahal Arax.

# PRE-GEN PCS

**Rahal Foramit**

*Rank:* 1

*Clock:* 1

*Faction Trait:* the way of the wolf (+2d6 when investigating someone's Edge)

*Signifier Edge:* I know when people aren't telling the whole story.

*Signifier:* a circle of wolf eyes

*Edge:* I pick up local customs quickly.

*Heresy:* I don't think the Hexarchate is living up to its own ideals.

**Rahal Thelne**

*Rank:* 1

*Clock:* 1

*Faction Trait:* the way of the wolf (+2d6 when investigating someone's Edge)

*Signifier Edge:* The grid is just another system to exploit.

*Signifier:* hands opposed as if to pry something open

*Edge:* I never forget a detail.

*Heresy:* My own sense of what is right should come first.

**Vidona Nuenor**

*Rank:* 1

*Clock:* 1

*Faction Trait:* the way of the stingray (+2 damage in unarmed combat)

*Signifier Edge:* I am a bastion for those who do not deserve to be hurt.

*Signifier:* the outline of an archaic castle

*Edge:* My pre-faction life was not entirely above the law.

*Heresy:* I will break the law to help those it harms without cause.

**Vidona Cressun**

*Rank:* 1

*Clock:* 1

*Faction Trait:* the way of the stingray (+2 damage in unarmed combat)

*Signifier Edge:* People often underestimate me.

*Signifier:* an unhatched egg

*Edge:* I'm always fighting to improve myself.

*Heresy:* I would give my life for my friends, but not for the Hexarchate.

# 2. POISON FROM WITHIN

**Factions:** Shuos, Kel
**Approaches:** stealth, combat

This adventure, the most heroic of the three, is designed to give the players a chance to take radical action—but at a cost.

## Overview

Although many of the leadership positions in the Hexarchate are held by members of various factions, the minor planet of Glivel is governed by a non-faction member, a woman named Thanda Mhai. She has achieved her place through her family's powerful network of political connections, and quite possibly some blackmail; opinion is divided as to whether her ultimate goal is to secure herself membership in a faction, or to maintain her independence while maximizing power for herself and her family. (Precisely which faction has appointed her to the governorship is left for the GM to choose, but it should not be the Shuos or the Kel.)

Her control over the planet, however, is less than entirely secure. For almost her entire tenure there, Thanda Mhai has been notorious for her struggle against an internal rebellion—a rebellion she quashes on a regular basis, and with noteworthy brutality. Despite these efforts, it seems the struggle continues unabated.

When the PCs arrive in the system, Mhai does not hesitate to use her political influence to have them placed at her disposal. Her stated goal is to have them eliminate the rebellion, on which she claims to have a lead. The truth is that Mhai is jumping at shadows, imagining insurrection everywhere she looks—and in the process, creating her own enemy. There is no rebellion; there is, however, a conspiracy to assassinate her, in the hopes that her replacement will be less paranoid and brutal. The PCs must first uncover this conspiracy, and then decide what to do about the conspiracy and the governor it is targeting.

## Setup

If the PC party is all-Kel or mixed Kel and Shuos, then they are part of the Kel military hierarchy, with any Shuos seconded to the Kel. An all-Shuos group is Shuos infantry instead. Either way, shortly after arriving in orbit around Glivel for resupply, they receive a message from their superiors ordering them to divert from their previous mission to aid Thanda Mhai. Information on her family and how she attained her position as governor is readily available from their superiors, if they inquire.

They meet Thanda Mhai at the governor's palace, an extensive and sumptuously decorated place that is nonetheless *very* heavily defended—enough so that one might expect her to be living on a contested border with an outside enemy, not deep within the Hexarchate's own systems. Before the PCs are allowed to see her, they are passed through layers of unnecessary security protocols—protocols which, **upon examination**, are very clearly flawed. The theatrical nature of the security is impressive (the PCs may not bring any weapons with them, unless they **succeed at hiding one**), but it reeks of someone whose paranoia outstrips her actual skill at assessing threat.

Upon reaching Mhai, she subjects the PCs to a long diatribe about the various insurgent cells she has rooted out and destroyed, and how they always keep coming back. None of it sounds especially impressive; **adroit conversation** rapidly makes it clear that there is no example of the insurgents achieving any victories against Mhai (a fact she attributes to her zealous opposition). After a tedious amount of this—which the GM is advised to largely summarize, lest the players grow bored!—she finally reaches her point: Mhai believes she has finally gathered intel on, if not the central command of the insurgency, then surely one of their more dangerous arms. Her own police forces are spread thin, though, which is why she has called for assistance from the Shuos and/or Kel.

Her lead directs the PCs to Hundred Horizons Imports: an obscure shop in the capital's affluent shopping district, one which specializes in selling offworld plants and animals as house decorations and pets. Mhai claims this is a cover for weapons smuggling, and dispatches the PCs to trace the shop's connections to the insurgency.

## Development

In pursuing Mhai's lead, the PCs can choose either a blunt-force approach, or a subtler path of counter-intelligence.

The blunt-force approach involves storming Hundred Horizons Imports and arresting the proprietor, a man named Ch'egh. (No check is required; Ch'egh has no hope of resisting even a single PC.) This provokes outcry from the neighbors, none of whom are armed, but all of whom insist on the proprietor's innocence. Mhai's behavior has made it clear she expects the PCs to brutally put down any such outcry as treasonous resistance against the governor, but in context that would blatantly be a massacre of defenseless civilians. The PCs may respond with violence (resolve with **a single unopposed check** from each player), but if the neighbors are harmed, convincing Ch'egh to talk becomes more difficult.

Upon having been arrested, the PCs can question Ch'egh. If the PCs have handled the protest without violence, they can **persuade him to talk** relatively easily, but if anyone was hurt, he gains the Edge "I will not tell these people anything." Ch'egh has heard nothing about an insurgency; all he can say is that he's been paid to deliver a rather bland-looking potted fern to the Rebounding Sky arena that night.

If the PCs pursue counter-intelligence instead, they can **eavesdrop** on Ch'egh's shop, **follow** his delivery servitors, or even attempt to **pass themselves off as his mysterious customers**. Success at any of these methods tells them a potted fern is to be delivered to the aforementioned location.

The Rebounding Sky arena is an indoor space used for a local sport, a kind of martial art performed in three dimensions on elastic cords—an odd location for a plant to be sent! Although the PCs may think the fern is code for something else or conceals a weapon within its pot, the plant is exactly what it appears to be. Further **querying of the grid** reveals that, when processed correctly, the spores of the fern can be used to make an extremely potent poison.

## Crisis

As before, the PCs can either choose to storm the arena or to infiltrate it. There are half again as many conspirators as there are PCs, led by an alt named Caadar.

Unlike Ch'egh's neighbors, these people are indeed armed and ready to protect themselves; any direct assault is a **battle**, albeit against opponents less effectively trained and armed than Shuos and Kel. (Treat all NPCs other than Caadar as having no Edges and half Health.) The conspirators' priority is to escape, and failing that, to die rather than be captured for questioning. If captured, like Ch'egh, they require **interrogation** before they will speak, with the Edge "We will not betray our friends." **Eavesdropping** on the meeting, by contrast, risks the conspirators escaping if they realize they're being observed, but increases the likelihood that the PCs will understand enough of the situation to make a conversation possible.

Whether the PCs eavesdrop or question at gunpoint, what they learn is that Mhai is not entirely wrong: there is indeed a conspiracy against her. However, it is not at all the widespread armed insurgency she so firmly believes is seeking to undermine her rule. Instead, the people at the arena are the entirety of the conspiracy, and their goal is much more precise. Caadar intends to take advantage of the flaws in Mhai's security to poison her wine with the processed spores of the fern, which are lethal enough to kill her before medicine can intervene. With Mhai removed, another governor will be assigned to replace her—one who, the conspirators hope, will be better for the people of Glivel.

Three main options are open to the PCs. They can do as Mhai wants and destroy the conspiracy, which leaves her in place as governor. It is extremely doubtful that the removal of this assassination plot will end her paranoia; instead she is likely to continue her brutally repressive policies, treating Glivel as her own personal fiefdom. Alternatively, they can allow the conspiracy to carry out its plan, eliminating Mhai. This does indeed result in a better governor being appointed. However, all the surviving conspirators are executed as heretics, along with their families and others closely associated with them, unless the PCs find a way to conceal the guilty parties or pin the blame on a scapegoat (for example, by doctoring Mhai's medical records to indicate an existing illness or allergy).

The third option—which the GM should not propose to the players, but can support if the players think of it independently—is for the PCs to assassinate Mhai themselves. With their superior skills and resources, they stand a better chance of getting away with it than the civilians do…but that outcome is by no means guaranteed.

Diplomatic solutions to this situation are unlikely to work. Mhai and the Thanda family are simply too well-connected; any attempt to remove her from office will fail in the face of their influence, and any attempt to persuade her to change her ways will have short-lived results at best.

The GM may also choose to have these outcomes affect the Hexarchate Clock. Destroying the conspiracy winds it up one step. If Mhai is assassinated and the conspirators are executed, the clock does not change; if Mhai is assassinated and the conspirators live, wind it down one step.

## Variations

Mhai's crimes against her own citizens may be detailed in more specific terms than generic "brutality." Those criminals she catches are often labeled heretics; the Hexarchate being essentially a theocratic society (with the high calendar standing in for its god), any crimes against the established order can be re-branded as heresy, even if they incorporated no attempt to diverge from the high calendar. Death as part of a remembrance is likely to include gruesome and baroque torture.

It is also up to the GM how to handle any hostile questioning of Ch'egh or the conspirators. Media often depicts torture as an effective means of gaining information, and it is plausible that the Kel in particular would subscribe to that belief; in reality, however, people subjected to torture are likely to say whatever they think will stop the pain, whether it's true or false. Shuos PCs might be aware of this dynamic and propose other methods, such as tricking the target into revealing information (e.g. by pretending to already know more than they really do) or offering clemency in exchange for cooperation.

If the PCs take action to hide the conspiracy or assassinate Mhai themselves, the GM may wish to extend the adventure with the arrival of a hex of Rahal investigators. How difficult it is to deceive the investigators should depend on how effectively the PCs carried out their crimes: one to two successes gives the Rahal the Edge "I suspect there's more to this story," while six or more successes gives the Rahal the Complication "I want to close this case as fast and quietly as possible."

## NPCS

**Thanda Mhai** (she/her)
Rank: non-faction
Clock: 2
*Signifier Edge:* As a scion of my family, I have deep roots in Glivel politics.
*Signifier:* A tree shaped like an hourglass, with roots as extensive as its branches.

*Edges:* My strong arm has a long reach.

I can browbeat almost anyone into doing what I want.

*Complication:* I've created my own nightmare and am terrified it'll destroy me.

**Caadar** (they/them)

Rank: non-faction

Clock: 2

*Signifier Edge:* I'm too clever for simple solutions.

*Signifier:* A winking monkey.

*Edges:* My silver tongue buys me all sorts of benefits.

I am an animate trove of botanical knowledge.

*Complication:* I'm part of a conspiracy to assassinate the governor, Thanda Mhai.

*Heresy:* Governance shouldn't be built on a pile of bones.

# PRE-GEN PCS

**Kel Issuem**

*Rank:* 1

*Clock:* 1

*Faction Trait:* the way of the hawk (+2d6 in physical combat)

*Signifier Edge:* My sacrifice won't be in vain.

*Signifier:* a bloodied soldier leaning on a weapon

*Edge:* My companions are my salvation.

*Heresy:* I won't follow orders that will get people killed for no good reason.

**Kel Nibor**

*Rank:* 1

*Clock:* 1

*Faction Trait:* the way of the hawk (+2d6 in physical combat)

*Signifier Edge:* My muscles alone make people reconsider their choices.

*Signifier:* a hawk perched atop a clenched fist

*Edge:* I can be surprisingly gentle with the young and the innocent.

*Heresy:* It isn't fair that the people with power are never the ones who pay the cost.

## Shuos Galheri

*Rank:* 1

*Clock:* 1

*Faction Trait:* the way of the fox (+2d6 when attempting to deceive someone or something)

*Signifier Edge:* People only notice me when I want them to.

*Signifier:* a whisper-thin outline of a fox

*Edge:* I am an expert in discreet violence.

*Heresy:* The bargain the Hexarchate makes with its citizens is too weighted in the Hexarchate's favor.

## Shuos Mahie

*Rank:* 1

*Clock:* 1

*Faction Trait:* the way of the fox (+2d6 when attempting to deceive someone or something)

*Signifier Edge:* I am a splendid distraction.

*Signifier:* a fox with fireworks exploding from its tails

*Edge:* I'm so good with the grid, I should have joined the Nirai.

*Heresy:* Ritual sacrifice is destroying our society and must be expunged.

# 3. THE FIELD OF DIPLOMACY

**Factions:** Andan, Nirai
**Approaches:** diplomacy, stealth

This adventure, the most complex of the three, is designed to give players a glimpse beyond the Hexarchate's borders.

## Overview

Approximately ten years ago, the Hexarchate came into contact with a foreign polity known as the Chutsomaa. Relations since then have been remarkably amicable, thanks in part to a form of technology the Chutsomaa developed, which they call the "embassy field." This technology—which is clearly either invariant or compatible with the high calendar, since the Chutsomaa are able to use it within Hexarchate territory—helps their emissaries adapt to the cultures of those they encounter. Thanks to its effects, they are able to speak the high language fluently and correctly interpret and respond to Hexarchate customs. (A diplomat equipped with this field would never, for example, wear fingerless gloves to a meeting with a Hexarchate representative, even if they don't know why.)

Dealings with the Chutsomaa have been spearheaded by a married couple, Andan Hidlao and Nirai Mithan, who met on the station. Hidlao manages the diplomatic interactions while Mithan provides support, assisted by a staff of other Hexarchate personnel. If this adventure is being run as an independent game or as the start of a longer campaign, the PCs have been part of that staff for long enough to get to know both Hidlao and Mithan; if this is an episode within a campaign, they have been seconded to the Chutsomaa border for the time being.

Hidlao's reputation is that of a deft and surprisingly gentle diplomat. He has managed good relations with the Chutsomaa, arranging a number of mutually beneficial exchanges and maintaining the Chutsomaa as an ally without using the Hexarchate's greater size and strength to force them into a subordinate position. Some in the Hexarchate leadership feel he's too soft on the heretic foreigners, but Hidlao's work has kept that border peaceful, allowing military resources to be allocated elsewhere.

The reality is that "Hidlao" is a Chutsomaa infiltrator—but not a malevolent one. The embassy field is far stronger than the Chutsomaa have admitted; it allows Hidlao to convince those around him that he is an Andan in good standing (though it does not bestow their faction ability on him). He has used this to maintain peace along the border for ten years, protecting his people against the Hexarchate.

Setting note: the Chutsomaa are a polity invented for this scenario, and nothing about their culture is detailed here. Depending on how the adventure is run, the specifics of Chutsomaa society need not be relevant, as their diplomat is adapting to Hexarchate customs. However, if the players are interested in digging further on that side, the GM may wish to flesh out the foreigners in greater depth.

## Setup

A delicate negotiation has recently begun. The Chutsomaa are facing some aggression from another neighbor (who are not themselves adjacent to the Hexarchate), and they are hoping to gain some non-military aid against that threat. The meeting is taking place on a station within Hexarchate space, and the PCs have been tasked to accompany and assist.

But they have a second mission as well. Andan Pesak, a more senior-ranking member of the faction, wants to learn more about the Chutsomaa's embassy field technology, which might be of use to the Hexarchate (since it functions in their territory). Thus far Andan Hidlao has been uncooperative, citing the Hexarchate's well-deserved reputation for first screwing over and then assimilating its neighbors; he thinks that attempting to pry into the matter would sour their currently good relations. Because of this, Pesak has asked the PCs to learn everything they can.

The Chutsomaa diplomat, Zorig khu Tsegal, enters with a machine built of graceful looping coils, about as large as a medium-sized dog, which they activate before greeting Andan Hidlao. Left to its own devices, the conversation between the two ambassadors runs smoothly, with Hidlao and Zorig drinking tea and exchanging poetry—the Andan way of negotiating. If the PCs **choose to participate**, they can learn that Zorig seems to consider Hidlao an old friend, and vice versa.

However, halfway through the meeting, any observant PC **has the chance to notice** that Zorig's machine seems to have stopped working: a small piece at the center that began rotating when activated has ceased to move. If this is pointed out to Zorig, they **attempt to brush it off** as not actually key to the machine's functioning. In reality (if the PCs see through their façade), Zorig is disturbed less by the machine breaking than by someone else noticing and bringing it up.

At no point during the meeting, before or after the machine breaks, does Zorig's facility with the high language or ability to negotiate Andan customs seem to falter. Even without technical skill, the PCs have sufficient reason to suspect that the machine does not work as they've been told. **Examining the machine's interaction with the local calendrical gradient** reveals that Zorig's device is nothing more than a pretty sculpture. With three or more successes, the investigating PC knows that *something* is active—some other, hidden device. However the embassy field operates, it is not what the Hexarchate has been told.

## Development

What happens next depends on who the PCs choose to report their observations to.

If they tell Andan Hidlao, he points out that it would be foolish of the Chutsomaa to show all their cards to the Hexarchate, and that taking precautions is not evidence of perfidy. He does, however, agree to speak with Zorig khu Tsegal about it, and offers to involve the PCs so their concerns can be laid to rest. This starts the PCs down the diplomacy path for this adventure.

If they consult with Nirai Mithan, she is troubled and agrees that the matter bears looking into—but not by confronting Zorig directly. She suggests instead that they attempt to covertly infiltrate the Chutsomaa ship and locate the real device, so they can analyze it and see if it poses any threat to the Hexarchate. This starts the PCs down the stealth path for this adventure.

If they send a message to Andan Pesak, it is clear that he considers the charade with the coiled device to be an act of covert aggression. He tells the PCs to secure an embassy field generator by any means necessary: demand it in exchange for Hexarchate assistance against the enemies of the Chutsomaa (diplomacy), or steal one for analysis and reproduction (stealth).

The PCs may attempt diplomacy first, following it up with stealth if that fails. Because this puts the Chutsomaa on their guard, however, the PCs all gain the Complication "They're on the lookout for us."

On the diplomacy path, **careful scrutiny of the conversation** between Hidlao and Zorig soon makes it obvious that Hidlao is not making any real attempt to gain information or concessions; any attempt to push in that direction rattles him. A sufficiently technical and stealthy PC can also **conduct calculations** that pinpoint the source of the exotic effect to something on Hidlao's wrist, hidden beneath his sleeve. If they are caught investigating, however, or if the two diplomats are **successfully confronted about their sham negotiations**, Zorig begins to defend Hidlao in a suspicious manner. Three or more successes in confrontation, or revealing knowledge about what Hidlao is wearing, provokes them into confessing the truth: that Hidlao is a Chutsomaa agent, aided by the real embassy field. They plead with the PCs to protect the mutually beneficial peace that has lasted all this time.

On the stealth path, the PCs must **bypass the Chutsomaa guards** to get on board the ship. Once there, they can **hack the Chutsomaa grid** to discover the general specs of the embassy field generator, which turns out to be a small, wearable device that can make someone into a near-flawless infiltrator. It seems to be designed for the wrist, but Zorig's sleeves were short enough in the previous meeting to confirm they wore no such thing. If the PCs know some device was at work before, process of elimination rapidly leaves them with only one conclusion: that Hidlao was the one with the Chutsomaa device. Alternatively, either Pesak or Mithan can confirm that he has always worn an interesting cuff on one wrist. The grid also inventories a second such device in Zorig's quarters; **going deeper into the ship** is a risk, but if successful, the PCs can steal that device.

Should the PCs be caught at any point on the Chutsomaa ship, the foreigners demand some form of apology. This results in Hidlao ending all investigation into the embassy field and deporting the PCs from the station; **political analysis** suggests he was only too ready to make that concession.

## Crisis

Given the number of pieces of information and technology the PCs might gain, and the number of interested parties involved, there are a large number of paths the ending of this adventure might follow. As with the previous adventures, these have the potential to affect the Hexarchate Clock, but the exact effects depend on who discovers how much.

The route most likely to wind up the clock is if Pesak is informed. At a minimum, if he is informed about the real nature of the embassy field, the Hexarchate's posture towards the Chutsomaa changes to an aggressive one, with an intent to overrun them militarily and assimilate them into the Hexarchate. If he gains an actual device, the clock winds up one step, as the Hexarchate can use it against their own citizens. If he further learns that Hidlao is a Chutsomaa agent, he immediately has Hidlao recalled and executed, and Mithan, whom Pesak assumes was a part of the conspiracy, is sent for reprocessing. This winds the clock up an additional step, as the Hexarchate goes to war. **Conceal-**

**ing any information from Pesak** is difficult, and any failed attempt could lead to severe negative consequences for the PCs.

If the PCs speak with Hidlao first, he insists his only desire is to maintain peace between the Hexarchate and the Chutsomaa. He volunteers to leave or even commit suicide to protect that peace, but if the PCs are in possession of a real embassy field device and he knows it, he will **attempt to destroy that first**, in order to prevent the Hexarchate from using it against his own people. This has no effect on the Hexarchate Clock. Sympathetic PCs can **persuade Hidlao to stay** and continue his work; this winds the clock down one step.

If they inform Mithan, she begs them to hold off on any action with Pesak while she confronts Hidlao. Any private meeting between them results in both vanishing (fled to the Chutsomaa). Should the PCs involve themselves in the conversation, though, they again have the option of **persuading the two to continue their work**, which again winds the clock down.

Any failure to provide an embassy field generator to Pesak, however, results in attitudes toward the Chutsomaa becoming more hostile...unless the PCs are able, perhaps with Mithan's help, to **craft a suitable decoy**—one that helps with understanding foreign customs, but cannot facilitate an infiltrator.

## Variations

The Chutsomaa as presented above are a relatively benign group, wanting only to protect themselves against the Hexarchate. However, the universe of in the Machineries of Empire series is one where few if any hands are clean: the Chutsomaa might well be guilty of repressive actions against their own people, or have a history of using their infiltrators to achieve less peaceful results than the one Hidlao has so far engineered. Although Hidlao himself is well-intentioned, the danger created by Zorig's false generator malfunctioning might mean Hidlao receives orders to begin working more actively against the Hexarchate—and his own wife.

This adventure particularly lends itself to operating as part of a longer campaign. If the Hexarchate gains a real embassy field generator, the PCs might be sent to infiltrate the Chutsomaa or some internal group their superiors hope to undermine. Alternatively, it is possible the PCs could take the device for themselves and use it against the Hexarchate!

## NPCS

**"Andan" Hidlao"** (he/him)

*Rank:* 3

*Clock:* 2

*Faction trait:* n/a; Hidlao is not actually an Andan

*Signifier Edge:* I can broker agreements where anyone else would fail.

*Signifier:* a wreath of new rosebuds

*Edges:* My gentle voice brings calm in tense situations.

I am a social infiltration specialist.

I have a clear view of both the Hexarchate and Chutsomaa.

*Complications:* I am a Chutsomaa spy disguised by the embassy effect.

I truly love my spouse, who is a loyal faction member.

**Nirai Mithan** (she/her)

Rank: 3

Clock: 2

*Faction Trait:* the way of the moth (wind up or wind down party or personal clock once per session)

*Signifier Edge:* My love of social sciences is an outlier among the Nirai.

*Signifier:* a moth among roses

*Edges:* I have an excellent grasp of logistics.

My friends and staff are loyal to me.

Together with my husband, I believe we can achieve great things.

*Complication:* I fear the peaceful situation I've helped create has a hidden, darker side.

*Heresy:* I want peace with the Chutsomaa, even if it costs the Hexarchate.

**Zorig khul Tsegal** (they/them)

*Rank:* non-faction

*Clock:* 2

*Signifier Edge:* I am an expert student of various cultures.

*Signifier:* flock of swallows flying together

*Edges:* I am a spymaster as well as a diplomat.

I am skilled in the use of technology compatible with the Hexarchate high calendar.

*Complications:* I know Hidlao is one of the Chutsomaa.

I fear I will fail my people, and we will be crushed as a result.

**Andan Pesak** (he/him)

*Rank:* 3

*Clock:* 3

*Signifier Edge:* I take other people's resources and power for myself.

*Signifier:* a rose vine strangling all within reach

*Edges:* Unlike many of my faction peers, I pay attention to technology.

I never let personal feelings sway me.

I am always on the lookout for betrayal.

*Complications:* My aggression often robs me of potential allies. I care more about my own advancement than the larger picture.

## PRE-GEN PCS

**Andan Lachel**

*Rank:* 1

*Clock:* 1

*Faction Trait:* the way of the rose (+2d6 when targeting an Edge in combat)

*Signifier Edge:* I can read people like an open book.

*Signifier:* a rose with stained glass petals that magnify all behind them

*Edge:* My presence puts people at ease.

*Heresy:* I hate that expression is not free in the Hexarchate.

**Andan Xef**

*Rank:* 1

*Clock:* 1

*Faction Trait:* the way of the rose (+2d6 when targeting an Edge in combat)

*Signifier Edge:* I adapt to different languages and cultures with ease.

*Signifier:* a rose growing on a stony mountain slope

*Edge:* No one suspects me of deception.

*Heresy:* The Hexarchate would be stronger if it believed in the possibility of peace.

**Nirai Rhada**

*Rank:* 1

*Clock:* 1

*Faction Trait:* the way of the moth (wind up or wind down party or personal clock once per session)

*Signifier Edge:* I instinctively understand exotic technologies.

*Signifier:* a moth whose wings are half-assembled puzzle pieces

*Edge:* I get along with servitors better than with people.

*Heresy:* There must be a better way to maintain the calendar than wasteful sacrifices.

**Nirai Kralt**

*Rank:* 1

*Clock:* 1

*Faction Trait:* the way of the moth (wind up or wind down party or personal clock once per session)

*Signifier Edge:* I'm just a nerdy technician, no threat to anyone.

*Signifier:* a moth blending into the background

*Edge:* I notice things that escape other people's attention.

*Heresy:* I would abandon the Hexarchate in a heartbeat if I thought anywhere else was better.

# APPENDIX A: CALENDRICAL TRAITS (OPTIONAL RULE)

Every day in the Hexarchate is governed by the high calendar, which assigns particular rules and rituals. These form Calendrical Traits that can be tagged on the appropriate day if the group is feeling creative.

To simulate this, for any given day, draw a card from a standard poker deck (Jokers removed) and consult the following table. The GM and players should improvise on the theme suggested by the holiday's name.

If a poker deck isn't ready to hand, you can simulate a card draw using a d4 (to determine the suit) and a d20 (to determine the card). On a d20, 1 = Ace, 2-10 are as normal, 11 = Jack, 12 = Queen, 13 = King, and reroll 14-20.

The GM and/or players should also feel free to generate a calendar of their own instead, or modify the one below.

**CLUBS (1 on a d4)**

A - The Festival of Dust Storms
2 - The Day of Masked Guards
3 - Celebration of the Victory at Bramble Fortress
4 - Dirge for Lost Ships
5 - The Procession of the Thousand Birds
6 - Autumn Parade
7 - The Drowned General's Parade
8 - The Day of Stifled Moths
9 - The Festival of Unwinnable Games
10 - The Day of Silicon Locusts
J - The Winter Migration
Q - The Blessing of Six Pyres
K - Anniversary of the Hexarchate's Founding

**DIAMONDS (2 on a d4)**

A - The Blessing of the Myriad Seeds
2 - The Jester's Triumph
3 - The Dance of Summer Tides
4 - The Day of Averted Eyes
5 - The Musicians' Gala
6 - Festival of Spring Blossoms
7 - The Day of Inverted Pleasures
8 - The Burning of Broken Clocks
9 - The Remembrance of Ashen Names
10 - The Day of Barefoot Dancing
J - Celebration of the Stars Unending
Q - Harvest Moon Feast
K - Accession of a New Hexarch

### HEARTS (3 on a d4)

A - Celebration of Children
2 - The Courtesans' Dance
3 - The Lovers' Gift Exchange
4 - Remembrance of Stillborn Friendships
5 - Recitations of Fertility and Flowers
6 - Mid-Year Poetry Festival
7 - The Festival of Thwarted Longings
8 - The Day of Braided Hopes
9 - The Gamblers' Revel
10 - Celebration of the Elders
J - The Feast of Comrades
Q - The Festival of Rare Wines
K - New Year's Gift Exchange

### SPADES (4 on a d4)

A - Mourning for Collapsed Stars
2 - The Lament of Fallen Poets
3 - The Appeasement of the Waters
4 - Remembrance of Hellspin Fortress
5 - Day of Silent Mourning
6 - Celebration of the Honored Dead
7 - The Day of Hollow Novas
8 - The Day of Sharpened Blades
9 - The Remembrance of Candle Arc
10 - The Feast of Shadow Victuals
J - The Procession of Bone Lanterns
Q - The Remembrance of Scoured Heretics
K - Year's End Meditation

# APPENDIX B: AN OVERVIEW OF THE HEXARCHATE

This is an overview of the Hexarchate as it appears in the author's books. It is intended as an **optional resource** due to the number of common triggers that appear or are implied. Feel free to modify anything and everything to make the setting suitable for you and your players. **Not all worldbuilding details are represented in the RPG's rules**—in particular, some faction traits have been modified in the RPG.

NOTE: Spoilers for the books follow.

## HIGH CALENDAR

The Hexarchate is governed by a consensus reality called the **high calendar**, which transcends the ordinary laws of physics. In fact, in this universe, the laws of physics change according to the calendar that is enforced, sometimes enabling wondrous effects like FTL, or the destructive power of terrible weapons.

The high calendar has twelve months, two for each faction. There are 30 days in a month, 30 hours in a day, 100 minutes in an hour, and 100 seconds in a minute. The months are as follows:

1 = Wolf

2 = Rose

3 = Fox

4 = Hawk

5 = Moth

6 = Stingray

7 = Wood

8 = Bells

9 = Eyes

10 = Pyres

11 = Stars

12 = Knives

# REMEMBRANCES

One of the more unpleasant features of the high calendar is its **remembrances**. Plainly put, these are special holidays during which heretics are tortured and sacrificed. The Hexarchate's citizens endure this because they are used to the custom and because the Hexarchate's most powerful physics-defying technologies, especially its most powerful weapons, depend on the high calendar—and because the Hexarchate is reasonably good at providing for ordinary citizens. Besides, the rival nations that surround the Hexarchate have their own calendars, and those aren't necessarily pleasant either.

## FACTIONS

Beyond that, the Hexarchate is divided into six factions, whose hexarchs (leaders) form an oligarchy. By custom the Rahal hexarch speaks first at the hexarchs' virtual conferences, and the factions are nominally divided into three high factions (Rahal, Shuos, and Andan) and three low factions (Nirai, Kel, and Vidona). However, the most powerful hexarch at a given point in time is usually determined by personality and faction resources, and changes over time as the hexarchs intrigue among themselves.

## ANDAN

The Andan special ability is **enthrallment**, which enables an Andan to hypnotize or mind-control someone of lower social status by making eye contact in person. The ability is not without its weaknesses: it works more effectively the better the Andan understands the target's personality, and it loses effectiveness with each subsequent use. Still, enthrallment is a fact of life for an Andan, and one of the reasons that an Andan is always seeking to improve their social position.

Typical Andan professions include diplomat, financier or other business positions, sex and therapy work (the Andan are generally held to make the best courtesans), artists, actors, and socialites. They are also responsible for the Hexarchate's interactions with foreigners and aliens. The Andan are the faction with the most liberal attitude toward body mods, partly so they can be on the cutting edge of fashion, partly so their agents can gather information with senses beyond the merely human. Of course, a typical Andan contact specialist is trained in ways to manipulate and bully foreigners and aliens into giving the

Hexarchate a lot of concessions. There's nothing like the Star Trek "Prime Directive" here.

## KEL

The life of a Kel soldier, from the lowliest private to a high general, is governed by **formation instinct**, which compels a Kel to follow orders from a higher-ranking Kel. Because of the potential for abuse, Kel Command punishes any fraternization between two (or more) Kel by execution. It also provides Kel soldiers outlets like libido suppressants, pornography, or (in the case of the officers) the services of sex workers, but "hawkfucking" (as it's known) has not entirely been suppressed.

The Kel are ruled by Kel Command, which is a hivemind located at a hidden starbase known as The Aerie. All the high generals are wired together in a single mind, of which the Kel hexarch is the highest-ranking. Alone of the hexarchs, the Kel hexarch refers to themselves as "we," using an archaic first person plural pronoun.

Kel infantry have neural implants and communicate over the connection during combat. Starship crew are wired for hivemind work, which doesn't necessarily make them more effective fighters, but is rather used as a way of suppressing heresy.

Kel uniforms are made of high-tech chameleonic fabric that can morph into different formality levels or camouflage at need. All Kel wear black gloves; traditionally the gloves are only removed in public for suicide missions, and in private for lovers. (Personnel from other factions who serve with the Kel wear gray gloves as a courtesy.) The Kel salute is right fist to left shoulder, and the military uses a ten-day week. A common custom is for the ranking officer to pass around a communal cup at high table during mess.

Kel companies in a regiment have standardized designations.

1 = Kestrel
2 = Swan
3 = Crow
4 = Heron
5 = Falcon
6 = Tern
7 = Magpie
8 = Egret
9 = Shrike
10 = Vulture

Kel officer ranks and insignia

Lieutenant = Circle
Captain = a talon with a bead of blood
Major = four claws
Lieutenant Colonel = Crescent Moon
Commander or Colonel = star
Tactical group commander = star and flame
Brigadier general = a feather pierced by one ring
Major general = a feather pierced by two rings
Lieutenant general = a feather pierced by three rings
General = wings
High general = wings and flame

A commander and a colonel are morally equivalent; a commander is, in Kel parlance, a colonel in charge of a warmoth (starship). The Kel military is a unified service, so the same ranks are used in all branches.

## LIOZH

The Liozh used to lead the Heptarchate, which preceded the Hexarchate. They were the ethicists, concerned especially with the ethics of government. When they contemplated a heretical form of governance called democracy, and began questioning the utility of the remembrances, the other factions turned on them and destroyed them.

The Liozh do not exist anymore, except in whispers and buried scraps of history; occasionally heretics try to resurrect their heresy, but none has so far survived the attempt.

For more details on the Liozh and setting a campaign during the Heptarchate era, *see* Appendix C.

## NIRAI

The Nirai are responsible for science, engineering, technology, and medicine in the Hexarchate. Individual Nirai are often apolitical. Alone among the factions, they are led in day-to-day matters by a false Hexarch, because the true Hexarch, Nirai Kujen (*see* Kujen's character sheet in Appendix D), is the nine-century-old immortal responsible for creation and maintenance of the high calendar. The false Hexarch may make their home wherever they like, while Kujen maintains a number of secret bases for his convenience.

A Nirai always knows what the local time is, which doesn't sound all that impressive until you realize that they will always be able to detect whether or not the high calendar is in alignment in a given location—and whether any heresy is present.

## RAHAL

The Rahal nominally run the Hexarchate from Wolf Hall, protect ordinary citizens, and make the laws. Because they're forever making fussy adjustments to the high calendar based on arcane computations, they tend to be good at math. They include magistrates, police, judges, legislators, and the bureaucrats that support the whole apparatus.

The Rahal calendrical ability is **scrying**, which enables a Rahal to dig around in the target's subconscious. This is hit-or-miss for interrogations in that any information is encoded in the target's personal language of symbols, but a trained Rahal can often unearth any dirty laundry the target is hiding. (It should be noted that the Hexarchate has no principle of "you're innocent until proven guilty.") Up to six Rahal (called a "hex") can cooperate in scrying a single target, which makes the effects of scrying more powerful.

## SHUOS

The Shuos are known for their love of games. Their headquarters is at the Citadel of Eyes, which is a starbase orbiting an inhabited planet. The planet itself is home to Shuos Academy Prime, foremost of the Shuos training schools.

One of the best-known Shuos Academy traditions is a yearly games competition with different categories. Cadets compete fiercely, as excellent results can launch a brilliant career and poor results can result in ignominy.

The Shuos often assassinate each other in order to move up the food chain. Assassination is the most common way to make a bid for the Hexarch's seat. It is a rare Shuos Hexarch who survives more than a decade.

Despite this, the Shuos don't just train assassins. The faction also includes cryptologists, bureaucrats, sex workers, spies, and hackers (called grid divers).

The Shuos are the only faction with no (known) calendar-based faction power, and this makes the rest of the Hexarchate very nervous.

## VIDONA

The Vidona are the most insular and conservative faction. They also tend to marry among themselves because the rest of the Hexarchate dislikes the reminder of their role in enforcing its rules and carrying out the remembrances, and fears their faction ability.

The Vidona calendrical ability is called **deathtouch**. A Vidona can kill someone just by touching them skin to skin. Granted, a gun will kill a target from a safe distance, but people are wary of the Vidona all the same.

Besides torturers, doctors, and police, the Vidona are responsible for the equivalent of primary/secondary education (K-12 in the USA)—in other words, indoctrination. Imagine school if the teacher was able to kill anyone who got out of line, and justify it as dealing with incipient heresy.

<u>Common Citizens</u>
The majority of the Hexarchate's citizens are ordinary people rather than faction members. In theory they are protected by the Rahal, but in practice an accusation of heresy usually ends tragically for the citizen in question. A faction member always outranks a common citizen.

# CULTURE

Culture in the Hexarchate, despite its leaders' best attempts, varies quite a bit from world to world, station to station, whether it involves cuisines or movements in the visual arts. The overall aesthetic is roughly "space East Asians." That said, there are uncountably many subcultures, some from people that the Hexarchate has conquered.

Sexual expression is weakly regulated in the Hexarchate, for good and ill. Sex work is not stigmatized, and courtesans in particular enjoy high prestige. Sexual orientation and identity are not a matter of great interest. Sex changes, like other body mods, are not particularly difficult. The Hexarchate recognizes three genders (male, female, alt [nonbinary]).

Hexarchate marriages emphasize a businesslike joining of property/prestige while offering companionship and (where applicable) raising children. You're not necessarily expected to find romance in a marriage, and it's not uncommon for one or more partners to seek romantic love or sex outside the marriage. The Kel in particular are prone to polyamorous marriages. Most children are genetically engineered and "crèche-born" from artificial wombs, although some subcultures still prefer physical pregnancy.

There is no expectation of a right to privacy in the Hexarchate. It's a surveillance state. The only privacy a citizen can have is what they make for themselves.

The concept of intellectual property, especially in the arts, is weak. The arts function more on a prestige/patronage basis.

The Hexarchate has all manner of games, from card and board games to sports to extensive virtual reality scenarios. Culturally important games include Go (called pattern-stones), a card game known as jeng-zai (a dystopian variant of Tarot), and dueling (which resembles épée fencing, but with energy swords known as calendrical swords).

## LANGUAGES

The Hexarchate is home to many languages. The lingua franca is called the high language. It does not inflect for number, and it has only a single non-gendered third person pronoun. Like Korean or Japanese, it has a number of honorifics and the verbs are marked by numerous formality levels.

Machine translation exists for other languages in the Hexarchate's sphere of influence, and for foreign languages used by powers that it interacts with regularly. It's generally reliable, although for delicate situations or cases where nuances of style are important, a human interpreter or translator is still preferred.

For simplicity's sake, the Hexarchate uses a lot of familiar swear words, but the vilest ones usually involve bestiality (e.g. "that spider-fucker"). Faction members tend to use their faction's oaths, e.g. "for love of fox and hound" for Shuos, "fire and ash" for Kel, or "for thorn's sake" for Andan.

## TECHNOLOGY

Much of the scut work in the Hexarchate, from manufacturing to manual labor to parts of child care, is handled by robots known as servitors. Servitors come in all sizes and are usually evocative of animals in form. While the Hexarchate's citizens know that servitors are capable of understanding and responding to human language, few of them think about the extent to which servitors are sentient. The servitors themselves have a society with factions of their own (called enclaves). Courtesy is extremely important to them, as well as the necessity of protecting themselves from human interference.

Starships in the Hexarchate are known as moths, and the duration of FTL travel between systems is usually measured in weeks. Some citizens are aware that the moths run on biotechnology. What very few realize, even among the Nirai, is that the moths are enslaved cyborg aliens—and that they're sentient, with a telepathy- and music-based culture of their own. Moths are capable of FTL flight on their own. The "FTL technology" that depends on the calendar is primarily a technological "harness" that puts them under human control. Moths themselves come from a different dimension, known to the Hexarchate as "gate space"; the Hexarchate is not aware of any surviving free moths.

Note: this RPG's rules set does not make provision for servitor or moth characters (or non-faction/foreign humans, for that matter) due to its focus on PCs who are complicit in the Hexarchate's tyranny.

The Hexarchate's starship-mounted weapons range from the fungal canister, which can destroy planetary ecosystems, to more conventional weapons such as rail guns, bombs, or missiles. Personal arms include fairly low-tech gunpowder-based firearms plus calendrical swords (energy swords) that have a nonlethal mode for dueling.

Medical technology is generally advanced. People typically live to be 150 or older. While people can certainly be killed, missing limbs or organs can be regenerated as long as there's access to medical care. People can be put into stasis if immediate care is not available.

Most citizens are equipped with neural implants known as **augments**, which allow them to access timekeeping functions, run personalized programs, and interface with computers and/or the setting's version of the internet cyberpunk-fashion. Computers tend to be everywhere, and most people are used to them handling everything from screening visitors to answering queries about prices at a local café.

# APPENDIX C: THE HEPTARCHATE

The books give little detail about the Heptarchate, which was the Hexarchate's precursor, and which had seven factions. This appendix includes some basic guidance if your group is interested in playing in that time period.

The Heptarchate is ruled by the Liozh with administrative assistance from the Rahal. Other factions' roles are largely the same, and the sacrifice of heretics is still a feature of the high calendar. However, the Liozh begin to ask whether it's possible to transition to a technological base and democratic government system *without* sacrifices. In the books' backstory, this leads to the other factions rising up to overthrow, destroy, and erase the Liozh. An RPG campaign set during this period could certainly have a different outcome.

While FTL travel exists due to the early harnessing and subjugation of voidmoths, the Heptarchate predates true machine sentience. There are robots, but intelligent servitors don't exist yet.

The Liozh faction becomes available for characters during this era. For an example Rank 1 Liozh PC, *see* Liozh Votta in Appendix D.

## LIOZH

Emblem: the mirrorweb/seven-legged spider
Motto: *every reflection is a truth*
Colors: white and gold
Faction trait: *the way of the mirror*
Additional +2d6 when tagging your signifier outside of combat.

The Liozh are philosophers and ethicists, and act as politicians and heads of government; during this time period, the Rahal serve as judges and administrators under Liozh leadership. The Liozh are responsible for weighing the cost of the Heptarchate's actions against potential gains.

**If you're playing a Liozh, you're signaling that you're interested in wrestling with thorny matters of national survival and governance, and what kinds of actions are morally justified in the name of the "greater good."**

The key here is to remember that the Liozh may be ethicists by profession, but their ethics run the gamut from ends-means utilitarianism to idealists dedicated to public service and egalitarianism—and they are ethicists who are *politicians*. Think "ethicist" as "someone who theorizes about ethical systems," some of which may or may not be "good" or "humane" as we recognize it. As such, they're the people who created the Heptarchate's tyranny in the first place.

The Liozh were destroyed by the other factions for attempting to introduce democratic reform. Some of them undoubtedly believed this would improve conditions in the Heptarchate and elsewhere. But some of them were cynical politicians looking to expand their faction's power base into the mass of unaffiliated citizens. The other six factions recognized the threat this posed to them and acted accordingly.

Liozh PCs who work well in this game are those whose beliefs lead them to struggle with the conflict between the status quo and the possibility of a better world. NPCs, of course, may have darker motivations.

What the Liozh think of other factions:

- Andan: Their smooth tongues mean they can't be trusted, but they make peaceful solutions possible when dealing with insurgents or foreign powers.

- Kel: The regrettable truth is that the reality of politics means that every nation needs an army.

- Nirai: Their technological "solutions" cause as many problems as they solve.

- Rahal: Government is impossible without *bureaucracy*. The linchpin of the realm.

- Shuos: If anything, even less trustworthy than the Andan. Too bad they're so good at making themselves indispensable.

- Vidona: Unjustly despised for doing the necessary work that other people aren't willing to.

What the Andan think of the Liozh:
- Hypocrites who talk a good line about doing what's "right" but fall down on the side of pragmatic geostrategic considerations when push comes to shove.

What the Kel think of the Liozh:
- They don't take Kel honor as seriously as they should; but Kel honor means following their lead.

What the Nirai think of the Liozh:
- It would sure be nice if they provided more funding, given that Nirai technology is the underpinning of the Heptarchate's trade and infrastructure.

What the Rahal think of the Liozh:
- The Liozh have been gradually offloading the actual work of government to the Rahal, which makes some of the Rahal wonder: who needs the Liozh?

What the Shuos think of the Liozh:
- Too busy arguing about abstract ideals to pay attention to the things that really matter, which is sometimes useful and sometimes a problem.

What the Vidona think of the Liozh:
- Every politician can be bought for the right price, and it's worth it if it holds together the Heptarchate's traditions.

# APPENDIX D: FIGURES FROM THE HEXARCHATE

Here are some sample NPCs drawn from the books and beyond. The GM should feel free to use/change them according to their needs. Alternately, if your group is interested in playing a campaign loosely based on the books, you could adapt some of these character write-ups or use them as inspiration for PCs.

NOTE: there are some heretic/non-faction/foreign/alien/robot *NPCs* listed as examples for the GM, because PCs may run into them in the larger setting. However, this game does not support heretic/non-faction/foreign/alien/robot *PCs*.

I haven't included characters' appearances, genders, gender identities, or sexual orientation (if any). The GM and/or players should assign these as they see fit. Don't worry about "canon."

If you haven't read the books, beware spoilers!

\*\*\*

Name: Ajewen Cheris
Faction: n/a (heretic, formerly a Kel)
Rank: 3
  TRAITS
Faction Trait: n/a
  Edge (8)
  *I can endure suffering that would drive others mad.*
  SIGNIFIER: *a phoenix with sheathed wings*
  Edge (8)
  *I excel at mathematics.*
  Edge (8)
  *I trained as a Kel soldier for many years.*
  Edge (8)
  *The Hexarchate's robots are secretly my allies.*
  Heresy
  *I swore to destroy the Hexarchate after it destroyed my army.*
  Complication
  *I triggered the genocide of my people, the Mwennin.*
  Health (8)
  Personal Clock: 3
Party Clock: ?

***

Name: Andan Eri
Faction: Andan
Rank: 1
  TRAITS

Faction Trait: *The way of the rose*
+2d6 when targeting an Edge in combat.

Edge (8)

*I can find common ground with anyone.*

SIGNIFIER: *a rose between two bears*

Edge (8)

*I have a nose for people's personal weaknesses.*

Heresy

*Even heretics have something to offer us, if we only listened to them.*

Health (8)

Personal Clock: 1

Party Clock: ?

\*\*\*

Name: Andan Tseya

Faction: Andan

Rank: 2

TRAITS

Faction Trait: *The way of the rose*
+2d6 when targeting an Edge in combat.

Edge (8)

*People find me enchanting.*

SIGNIFIER: *a rose and a wineglass*

Edge (8)

*Computers hold no secrets from me.*

Edge (8)

*I am a trained assassin.*

Heresy

*If the Hexarchate is no longer able to survive in its original form, maybe it's time for something new.*

Complications

*I long for the approval of my mother—the Andan Hexarch.*
*I am an outcast among the Andan.*

Health (8)

Personal Clock: 2

Party Clock: ?

\*\*\*

Name: Andan Zhe Navo

Faction: Andan

Rank: 3

TRAITS

Faction Trait: *The way of the rose*

+2d6 when targeting an Edge in combat.

Edge (8)

*My presence inspires people to become their best selves.*

SIGNIFIER: *a shining silver rose*

Edge (8)

*As a poet, I understand the uses of propaganda and media.*

Edge (8)

*My study of history's lessons helps me see trends and traps in the present.*

Edge (8)

*I am a formidable tactician.*

Heresy

*The Heptarchate has lost sight of its vision of a just, prosperous world for everyone, and it's up to people like me to guide it back.*

Complications

*My brother's failed political maneuvers resulted in my own fall from grace among the Andan.*

*No one expects me to survive my political appointment as a general.*

Health (8)

Personal Clock: 4

Party Clock: ?

\*\*\*

Name: Hemiola

Faction: n/a (servitor)

Rank: 1

TRAITS

Faction Trait: n/a

Edge (8)

*I am a skilled composer and videographer.*

SIGNIFIER: *a music clef*

Edge (8)

*As a robot, I can interface easily with computers.*

Heresy: n/a

Complication

*I betrayed my master, Hexarch Nirai Kujen.*

*I am naïve about the way the Hexarchate works.*

Health (8)

Personal Clock: 2
Party Clock: ?

***

Name: Kel Brezan
Faction: Kel
Rank: 2
TRAITS
Faction Trait: *The way of the hawk*
+2d6 in physical combat.
Edge (8)
*I have a gift for independent action despite being a Kel.*
SIGNIFIER: *a phoenix sundered into many pieces*
Edge (8)
*I can identify people by their unique body language.*
Edge (8)
*I cannot tell a lie.*
Heresy
*I believe the Hexarchate can and should become a better version of itself.*
Complications
*I am estranged from my family for acting against the Hexarchate.*
*I have a hair-trigger temper.*
Health (8)
Personal Clock: 2
Party Clock: ?

***

Name: Kel Khiruev

Faction: Kel

Rank: 4

TRAITS

Faction Trait: *The way of the hawk*

+2d6 in physical combat.

EDGE (8)

*I have a gift for engineering.*

SIGNIFIER: *a phoenix holding a hammer in its talons*

EDGE (8)

*I have long experience leading armies.*

EDGE (8)

*I cultivate expertise and interest in high culture, especially music.*

EDGE (8)

*I am a tenacious negotiator.*

EDGE (8)

*Death doesn't frighten me.*

Heresy

*The Hexarchate should recognize heretics and robots as people, with the protections due to people.*

Complications

*I watched my Vidona mother kill my heretic father and it traumatized me.*

*I deliberately seek out relationships doomed to failure.*

Health (8)

Personal Clock: 3

Party Clock: ?

***

Name: Kel Tarun
Faction: Kel
Rank: 1
   TRAITS
Faction Trait: *The way of the hawk*
   +2d6 in physical combat.
   EDGE (8)
   *I will do anything for my comrades.*
   SIGNIFIER: *three phoenixes flying in formation*
   EDGE (8)
   *I can drive, ride, or pilot any vehicle ever built.*
   Heresy
   *Treating people fairly is more important than the Hexarchate's so-called principles.*
   Health (8)
   Personal Clock: 1
Party Clock: ?

***

Name: Liozh Votta
Faction: Liozh
Rank: 1
   TRAITS
Faction trait: *the way of the mirror*
   Additional +2d6 when tagging your signifier outside of combat.
   Edge (8)
   *People find it easy to trust me.*
   SIGNIFIER: *a jeweled spider at the heart of a web*

Edge (8)
*I have business connections everywhere I go.*
Heresy
*The Heptarchate would be more prosperous if it eased its treatment of foreigners and heretics.*
Health (8)
Personal Clock: 1
Party Clock: ?

***

Name: Moroish Nija
Faction: n/a (Hexarchate citizen, unaffiliated)
Rank: 1
TRAITS
Faction Trait: n/a
Edge (8)
*I am an accomplished thief.*
SIGNIFIER: *a broken lock*
Edge (8)
*I have a second sense for danger.*
Heresy
*People don't deserve to be wiped out for the Hexarchate's convenience.*
Complications
*I belong to the Mwennin, a minority people nearly wiped out by the Hexarchate.*
*The Shuos have taken an interest in my fate.*
Health (8)

Personal Clock: 2
Party Clock: ?

\*\*\*

Name: Nirai Areth
Faction: Nirai
Rank: 1

TRAITS

Faction Trait: *The way of the moth*

Once per session, **wind up** or **wind down** the party clock or your personal clock.

Edge (8)

*I am an expert in codes and ciphers.*

SIGNIFIER: *a moth drawn in 1's and 0's*

Edge (8)

*People don't notice me unless I want them to.*

Heresy

*The Hexarchate would benefit from new ideas and innovations—not just in technology, but in its government.*

Health (8)

Personal Clock: 1

Party Clock: ?

\*\*\*

Name: Nirai Kujen
Faction: Nirai
Rank: 6 (Hexarch)

TRAITS

Faction Trait: *The way of the moth*

Once per session, **wind up** or **wind down** the party clock or your personal clock.

**Special:** Once every six sessions, roll 1d6. If it comes up 6, wind up the Hexarchate clock.

Edge (8)

*I can cheat death by jumping to and possessing another body anywhere within the Hexarchate.*

SIGNIFIER: *a kaleidoscope of fluttering moths*

Edge (8)

*I control unimaginable wealth and luxury.*

Edge (8)

*I have mastered the eldritch sciences of the Hexarchate.*

Edge (8)

*My paranoia knows no bounds.*

Edge (8)

*I control secret bases scattered throughout the Hexarchate.*

Edge (8)

*I am nine hundred years old and I remember histories that everyone else has forgotten.*

Edge (8)

*I will do anything to survive.*

Heresy

n/a

Complications

*I no longer understand the chains of conscience.*
*I am shackled by my own luxuries.*
*I am terrified of true death.*

Health (8)

Personal Clock: 5
Party Clock: ?

\*\*\*

Name: Nirai Weniat
Faction: Nirai
Rank: 2

TRAITS

Faction Trait: *The way of the moth*

Once per session, wind up or wind down the party clock or your personal clock.

Edge (8)

*I am an expert at the Hexarchate's technologies of war.*

SIGNIFIER: *a moth resting on a gun*

Edge (8)

*Extremes of destruction and horror don't bother me.*

Edge (8)

*I'm hard to intimidate.*

Heresy

*I will protect my own people, even if it means coming into conflict with the Hexarchate's dictates.*

Complication

*I underestimate people who can't keep up with me in technical matters.*

*People find my callousness off-putting.*

Health (8)

Personal Clock: 4

Party Clock: ?

\*\*\*

Name: Rahal Mistrikor
Faction: Rahal
Rank: 1

TRAITS

Faction Trait: *The way of the wolf*

+2d6 when investigating someone's Edge.

Edge (8)

*I am a student of the Hexarchate's legal systems and loopholes.*
SIGNIFIER: *a wolf holding a scroll in its jaws*

Edge (8)

*I cultivate underground contacts with robots.*

Heresy

*The best way to overturn the Hexarchate's injustices is by reforming its laws from within.*

Complication

*My idealism sometimes gets the better of me.*

Health (8)

Personal Clock: 2

Party Clock: ?

\*\*\*

Name: Rahal Zaniin
Faction: Rahal
Rank: 3

TRAITS

Faction Trait: *The way of the wolf*

+2d6 when investigating someone's Edge.

Edge (8)

*Fear? What fear?*

SIGNIFIER: *a wolf with bared teeth*

Edge (8)

*I have mastered the mathematics of the high calendar.*

Edge (8)

*I am good at political maneuvering.*

Edge (8)

*I thrive when it comes to debate and persuasion.*

Heresy

*Protecting lives is more important than the Hexarchate's dogma.*

Health (8)

Personal Clock: 3

Party Clock: ?

\*\*\*

Name: The *Revenant*

Faction: n/a (the *Revenant* is a voidmoth—a sentient alien cyborg starship)

Rank: 3

TRAITS

Faction Trait: n/a

Edge (8)

*I will stop at nothing to seize freedom.*

SIGNIFIER: *a shattered chain*

Edge (8)
*My plans are devious.*
Edge (8)
*I have robot allies.*
Edge (8)
*I control the most powerful ship-mounted weapon known to the Hexarchate, the shear cannon.*

As far as ship-to-ship combat goes, the shear cannon should be considered a one-hit-kill plot weapon that can be used once a session. The *Revenant* also comes with FTL capability. Make sure the PCs understand this if they come into conflict with it!

Heresy

n/a

Complication

*Having been created as a tool for human conquest, I don't trust humans.*

\*\*\*

Name: Shuos Jedao
Faction: n/a (heretic, formerly Shuos)
Rank: 4

Jedao has dyscalculia and compensates using computer aid.

TRAITS

Faction Trait: n/a

Edge (8)
*I always have a plan.*
SIGNIFIER: *a nine-tailed fox crowned with eyes*

Edge (8)
*I'm good at reading people.*
Edge (8)
*I excel at manipulating people.*
Edge (8)
*I am an expert at violence in all its forms.*
Edge (8)
*I am a master of games.*
Heresy
*I swore to destroy the Hexarchate after my lover was executed for heresy.*

Complications
*People fear me because I once massacred my own army.*
*I am immortal yet I long for death.*
*I have abysmal taste in lovers.*

Health (8)
Personal Clock: 4
Party Clock: ?

\*\*\*

Name: Shuos Mikodez
Faction: Shuos
Rank: 6 (Hexarch)

Mikodez has ADHD and uses drugs to manage the symptoms.

TRAITS

Faction Trait: *The way of the fox*

+2d6 when attempting to deceive someone or something

Edge (8)

*I am a master of persuasion.*

SIGNIFIER: *a smiling fox*

Edge (8)

*People's hearts are like an open book to me.*

Edge (8)

*People are afraid of crossing me.*

Edge (8)

*I command the loyalty of my organization.*

Edge (8)

*I see the big picture.*

Edge (8)

*I have an ear in every corner of the Hexarchate.*

Edge (8)

*I have an instinct for choosing the winning side.*

Edge (8)

*I take care of my people.*

Heresy

*The Hexarchate's ritual sacrifices are a waste of human resources.*

Complications

*I am notorious for assassinating the other hexarchs.*

*I am in mourning because I sent my brother to his death.*

Health (8)

Personal Clock (5)

Party Clock (?)

\*\*\*

Name: Shuos Yeren

Faction: Shuos

Rank: 1

   TRAITS

Faction Trait: *The way of the fox*

   +2d6 when attempting to deceive someone or something.

   Edge (8)

   *I can hack into any computer system.*

   SIGNIFIER: *a fox trailing lightning*

   Edge (8)

   *I connect easily with other people.*

   Heresy

   *The Hexarchate/Heptarchate should explore less cruel methods of social control.*

   Complication

   *My best friend and my lover were implicated in heresy and treason.*

   Health (8)

   Personal Clock (3)

Party Clock (?)

***

Name: Shuos Zehun

Faction: Shuos

Rank: 5

   TRAITS

Faction Trait: *The way of the fox*

   +2d6 when attempting to deceive someone or something.

Edge (8)

*My loyalty to Hexarch Mikodez is beyond question.*

SIGNIFIER: *a guardian nine-tailed fox*

Edge (8)

*I can organize anything.*

Edge (8)

*I know where all the secrets of the Shuos are buried.*

Edge (8)

*I have an excellent memory.*

Edge (8)

*I used to be an instructor at Shuos Academy Prime.*

Edge (8)

*The Shuos walk carefully around me.*

Heresy

n/a

Complications

*I am enraptured by my pet cats.*
*Old age is catching up to me.*

Health (8)

Personal Clock (4)

Party Clock (?)

***

Name: Vahenz afrir dai Noum

Faction: n/a (foreigner of unknown origin)

Rank: 3

TRAITS

Faction Trait: n/a

Edge (8)
*I am adept at political manipulation.*
SIGNIFIER: *a knife with a silken tassel*
Edge (8)
*I am a master strategist.*
Edge (8)
*I am versed in the tools of spycraft.*
Edge (8)
*I can adapt to any culture.*
Complication
*I underestimate my opponents.*
*I have few real friends because of my own paranoia.*
Health (8)
Personal Clock: 4
Party Clock: ?

\*\*\*

Name: Vidona Elpen
Faction: Vidona
Rank: 1
TRAITS
Faction Trait: *The way of the stingray*
+2 damage in unarmed combat.
Edge (8)
*I work loopholes to my advantage.*
SIGNIFIER: *a stingray tangled up with a ribbon*
Edge (8)
*I am good at bluffing.*

Heresy

*No one expects a saboteur against the Hexarchate in the very midst of the Vidona.*

Health (8)

Personal Clock: 1

Party Clock: ?

\*\*\*

Name: Vidona Oressa

Faction: Vidona

Rank: 3

TRAITS

Faction Trait: *The way of the stingray*

+2 damage in unarmed combat.

Edge (8)

*I have mastered the medical arts.*

SIGNIFIER: *a stingray and a needle*

Edge (8)

*I have incredible strength of will.*

Edge (8)

*I don't care what others think of me.*

Edge (8)

*I have contacts outside the Hexarchate who owe me favors.*

Heresy

*Everyone deserves a place where they can thrive—even if they're heretics, and that place is outside the Hexarchate.*

Complication

*The Vidona, my own faction, dislike my advocacy for fair treatment of prisoners.*

Health (8)

Personal Clock: 4

Party Clock: ?

\*\*\*

Name: Vidona Senar

Faction: Vidona

Rank: 3

TRAITS

Faction Trait: *The way of the stingray*

+2 damage in unarmed combat.

Edge (8)

*My intimate knowledge of anatomy and physiology makes me a deadly fighter.*

SIGNIFIER: *a stingray and a sword*

Edge (8)

*I maintain backdoor access to all the Vidona's records and surveillance.*

Edge (8)

*People find me intimidating.*

Edge (8)

*I lead a secret existence as a vigilante.*

Heresy

*I use my skills as a Vidona and my access to their resources to save the innocent person by person.*

Personal Clock: 3
Party Clock: ?

# ACKNOWLEDGMENTS

Thank you to Android Press, my agent Seth Fishman, and Jack Gernert for making this project a reality.

Thanks to the following people for their comments, mentorship, and assistance: Sam Kabo Ashwell, Arabelle Betzwieser, Joseph Betzwieser, Marie Brennan, Chris Chinn, Stephanie Folse, David Gillon, Toby Leonard, Elizabeth McCoy, Redsixwing, and Ursula Whitcher.

Special thanks to the following playtesters: Raye Cochran, Diana Jakobs, Starstreaker, and Redsixwing.

Last but not least, thank you to the lovely readers of Machineries of Empire for your encouragement and support. I hope you enjoy the game!

Yours in calendrical heresy,

Yoon Ha Lee

# ABOUT THE AUTHOR

A Korean-American sf/f writer who received a B.A. in math from Cornell University and an M.A. in math education from Stanford University, Yoon finds it a source of continual delight that math can be mined for story ideas. Yoon's novel *Ninefox Gambit* won the Locus Award for best first novel, and was a finalist for the Hugo, Nebula, and Clarke awards; its sequels, *Raven Stratagem* and *Revenant Gun*, were also Hugo finalists. His middle grade space opera *Dragon Pearl* won the Mythopoeic Award for Children's Literature and the Locus Award for best YA novel, and was a New York Times bestseller. Yoon's short fiction has appeared in publications such as *Tor.com*, *Clarkesworld Magazine*, and *Audubon Magazine*, as well as several year's best anthologies.

Yoon's hobbies include composing music, art, and destroying the reader. He lives in Louisiana with his family and an extremely lazy catten.

www.ingramcontent.com/pod-product-compliance
Ingram Content Group UK Ltd.
Pitfield, Milton Keynes, MK11 3LW, UK
UKHW021455280925
8114UKWH00027B/511